Lexi Catt's Meowmoirs—Tales of Heroic Scientists

LEXI AND IMHOTEP
To the Rescue

By Marian Keen

Illustrated by Jodie Dias and Wendy Watson
Edited by Nancy Wickham

First Published in Canada 2015 by Life Journey Publishing

Editor: Nina Shoroplova
Assistant Editor: Susan Kehoe
Production Editor: Jennifer Kaleta
Story Development Editor: Jodie Dias
Development Editor: Nancy Wickham
Illustrators: Jodie Dias, Wendy Watson
Cover Illustration: Jodie Dias, Wendy Watson
Book Cover Design: Marla Thompson
Typeset: Greg Salisbury
Photographer: Wendy Watson

DISCLAIMER: *Lexi and Imhotep* is an historical fiction story for children. While much of the story has been well researched, and is based on true events and people who lived during the era of the story, the story itself is a work of fiction based on the author's imagination. Parents, teachers, and children may use the information in the book's "Pawscript" as an informative and factual resource. Readers of this publication agree that neither Marian Keen nor her publisher will be held responsible or liable for damages that may be alleged or resulting directly or indirectly from the reading of this publication.

Dedicated to
Creative thinkers—past, present, and future—who study
history, learn from it, and then with courage break new
ground to build a better civilization.

*Greatness is not a national, but an individual phenomenon ... all men
are brothers in their weaknesses, if in nothing else.*
~ Barbara Mertz

TESTIMONIALS

"Marian Keen has done it again in this newest story in her series about Lexi Catt and his adventures throughout history. From his antics as a spunky kitten to his journey down the Nile with Hotep and Genie to meet Pharaoh Ramses II, readers will enjoy every fun-filled page. The illustrations bring ancient Egypt to life, and the "Pawscript" at the back of the book is very helpful and informative for middle-grade readers who are experiencing new vocabulary and learning about the lifestyles and events of ancient Egypt."

Samantha Watson, Special Education,
New Westminster and Maple Ridge School Districts

ACKNOWLEDGEMENTS

I wish to express sincere appreciation to John Dias for the inspiration and concept of the *Lexi Catt Series*, which brings to life the history of science and medicine. Alexander Catt II, also known as Lexi, is a spunky spokes-feline who allows me to share my interest in the health sciences with children. Thank you, John, for opening the door to these exciting adventures.

Researching ancient Egypt—a culture 5,000 years old with a language long dead—would be near impossible if not for those who have studied and shared their knowledge about this era. I am indebted to many historian authors and especially acknowledge Barbara Mertz, PhD, and Carole Reeves, PhD, for their amazing books on the subject.

I wish to thank Julie Salisbury and her team at Influence Publishing, especially publication editor Nina Shoroplova, for the opportunity to bring Lexi's eye on history to young readers. Children now have the chance to become acquainted with some true heroes of history.

I wish to thank my daughters, Jodie Dias and Wendy Watson, for bringing the story to life with charming, whimsical visuals, while maintaining historical truth.

I wish to thank Nancy Wickham for her meticulous attention to detail and clarity in editing my written words and her patience in dealing with my cockeyed humour.

I want my family to know that I appreciate their patience and support in this endeavour by never complaining about the long hours I spend on this project.

PREFACE

Introducing readers to scientists who have made a difference throughout human history has been a challenging but satisfying venture.

The purpose of the series *Lexi Catt's Meowmoirs—Tales of Heroic Scientists* is twofold. One is to share some of the amazing accomplishments in the health sciences from ancient Egypt to modern times. And the second is to show readers the struggles as well as the inspirations, the perseverance as well as the courage integral to these individual scientists and doctors. The research necessary to accomplish this has been inspiring.

The story of *Lexi and Imhotep to the Rescue*, however, presented a unique challenge.

Imhotep was the most-honoured physician, vizier, and architect of Pharaoh Djoser's Third Dynasty. He was talented in many fields—he saved the kingdom from a seven-year drought; he built the first pyramid of stone; and he wrote many medical texts. He was so important to the Egyptians that they deified him one thousand years after his lifetime.

So while no series about historical medicine and science would be complete without including ancient Egypt and honouring Imhotep, the information from the period of the Third Dynasty is too sparse to depict his actual lifetime.

This is why I have chosen to create a story of his imagined descendant Imhotep ("Hotep" for short) living in the era of Ramses the Great—Ramses II—for which there are plenty of historic materials and current writing enabling me to show daily life, travel, and even the details of medical treatments.

Most of the medical treatments in the story have come from ancient Egyptian records such as the Ebers Papyrus, which is believed to have been written by the famous Imhotep, god of medicine and healing. My fictional character "Hotep" embodies the attributes of Imhotep of the Third Dynasty—intelligence, leadership, compassion, and hard work.

I have also created the character Hygenia, a young woman, who, like Hotep, is studying in Karnak to become a physician. Her name is based on Hygieia, the Greek goddess of health and hygiene. Hotep's mother is named Mayet (an Egyptian name meaning "kitten"), and Hygenia's pet asp is named Khleo, using the old Egyptian way of spelling "Cleo."

I have chosen to focus on the development of the practice of medicine within the ancient Egyptian civilization. Egyptian culture peaked at the time of Ramses II with plenty of records in tombs, temples, monuments, and *stelae*; Egyptologists have provided a feast for a storyteller to work from.

Come. Join Lexi as he helps young Hotep in a dangerous rescue operation and solves a mystery in his feline way.

TABLE OF CONTENTS

LIST OF ILLUSTRATIONS

Lexi Catt
Map of Ancient Egypt
Revenge was sweet!

Lexi Catt

LEXI CATT'S MEOWMOIRS

My name is Alexander Catt II, but people call me Lexi. I was born in Luxor, Egypt, during Ramses II's reign as Pharaoh. My father was Alexander Catt, the adventurer, and my mother was called Ebony. I am all black like my mother, but I have a white muzzle, white paws, and a small tip of white on my talented tail. I have already lived eight of my nine lives, and my *purr*pose now is to write the *tails* of my adventures in my *meow*moirs like my father wrote his before me.

I have a peculiar attraction to trouble. Fortunately, the strange twitch of my tail warns me when trouble is near. For this reason, I have always tried to live with scientists or doctors of medicine over the centuries. You never know when you need a doctor in the house!

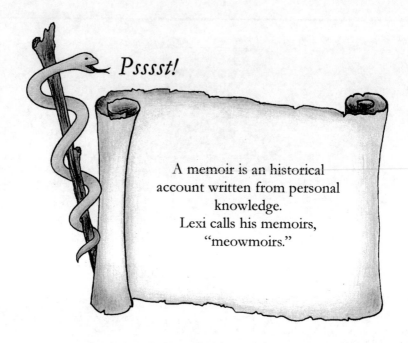

Psssst!

A memoir is an historical
account written from personal
knowledge.
Lexi calls his memoirs,
"meowmoirs."

In this *tail* of adventure, I live with a young man named
Imhotep, who was named after his ancestor—Egypt's famous
doctor, Imhotep. Young Hotep studies diligently to become a
doctor and to live up to the name of the great Imhotep. He
and I live during the reign of Ramses II, and our travels take
us to the Valley of the Kings, to Deir el-Medina, and down the
Nile River to meet the Pharaoh himself!

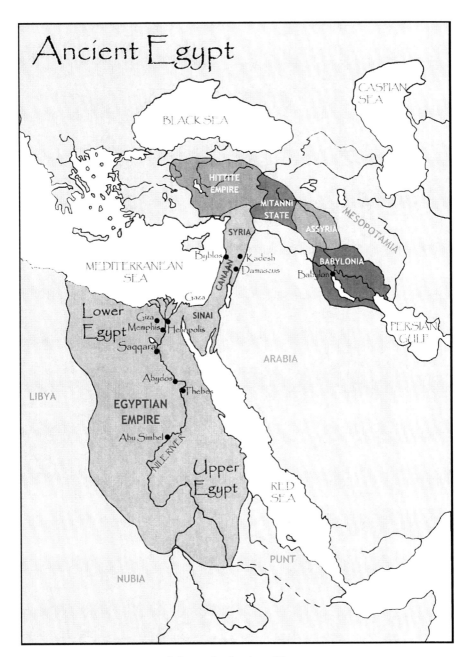

Ancient Egypt

CASPIAN
SEA

BLACK SEA

HITTITE
EMPIRE

MITANNI
STATE

MESOPOTAMIA

SYRIA

ASSYRIA

Byblos

Kadesh

BABYLONIA

MEDITERRANEAN
SEA

CANAAN

Damascus

Babylon

Gaza

PERSIAN
GULF

Lower
Egypt

Giza

SINAI

Memphis

Heliopolis

Saqqara

ARABIA

LIBYA

Abydos

Thebes

EGYPTIAN
EMPIRE

Abu Simbel

NILE RIVER

Upper
Egypt

RED
SEA

PUNT

NUBIA

Map of Ancient Egypt

Revenge was sweet!

Chapter One

My Life with Hotep Begins

In 1264 BCE, Luxor, Egypt, there were no sirens or horns. Life was quiet—dull even. When I was a little kitten, as soon as I could see I made for the open door, evading Mama Ebony's watchful eye. What I saw was astonishing. A big yellow ball hung in the west and the sky was red. The adobe walls looked as if they were on fire. My black and white fur stiffened. I wanted to be part of that exciting world. I stretched out a white paw, ready to take my first step into trouble!

"Lexi! You imp!" Mama grabbed my scruff and I was back with my brothers in a blink.

"You'll find out soon enough how dangerous it is out there!" scolded Mama who was pretty scary herself. She was the proverbial all-black cat—just like Bastet.

"Mewy! Mewy!" laughed my brothers, who had ratted on me to Mama. I closed my eyes and planned my revenge on them.

The cooking yard was a dangerous place. Mama kept telling us to stay away; so, of course, I continued to sneak out there and convinced my brothers it was amazing! It smelled so good that they finally came. They sat like scared rabbits in the corner, and I watched for my chance!

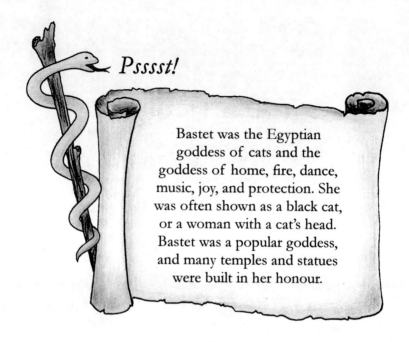

Psssst!

Bastet was the Egyptian goddess of cats and the goddess of home, fire, dance, music, joy, and protection. She was often shown as a black cat, or a woman with a cat's head. Bastet was a popular goddess, and many temples and statues were built in her honour.

The young boy who helped with the cooking always had a bit of difficulty with the heavy water jug. He was trying to carry the water jug across the yard to the cook. I ran past him, dug my tiny claws into his foot, and was back to our nest in a wink. The poor boy cried out, lost his balance, and spilled the water on my brothers. *Mewy! Mewy!* Revenge was funny and so sweet!

"Scorpion! Scorpion! I've been stung!" cried the boy.

"There's no scorpion," scolded the cook, but she saw a spot of blood. "It's merely a flea bite. We'll have to fumigate with fleabane with these cats attracting the fleas." She shooed my brothers, soaking wet and mewing, out of the cooking yard. Mama caught them and cuffed them back to bed. I pretended to be asleep!

Big, tall, gentle, loving Hotep

One day in the alley behind the cooking yard, I saw the same boy drop a bundle of reeds. They bounced and rolled with quite a clatter. As he gathered them up to tie them, I spotted one he'd missed and I gave it a good push towards him. *Yeow!* What pain! A splinter of the reed went right into my paw. I mewed and mewed in pain.

That's when Imhotep appeared. He had just come home from school at Karnak. He picked me up … and up and up and up! Hotep was tall! I was so scared, I yeowed even louder. With my speared paw I didn't have enough courage to leap!

Gently, Hotep took my paw and drew out the reed splinter. He firmly pressed the bleeding hole in my paw with his thumb and middle finger. He held the pressure as he stroked my fur and, bit by bit, I felt better. It was then I started to love big, tall, gentle, loving Hotep.

Psssst!

Karnak is a city full of temples. It is one of the world's largest religious sites with over twenty-five temples and chapels and a sacred lake on its two hundred acres. Thirty Pharaohs added to the complex during their reigns, spanning two thousand years.

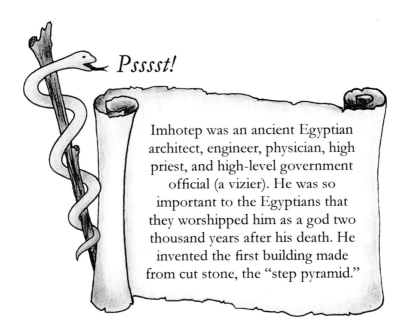

Psssst!

Imhotep was an ancient Egyptian architect, engineer, physician, high priest, and high-level government official (a vizier). He was so important to the Egyptians that they worshipped him as a god two thousand years after his death. He invented the first building made from cut stone, the "step pyramid."

Mayet, the lady of the house, entered the kitchen. She said, "Hotep! You're home!"

She stood on tiptoe as he bent down for her kiss.

"Yes, Mother, I came home for the holiday. I see Ebony has had kittens. This one had a sliver in his paw. I took it out just now and he seems fine."

"That's good. His name is Lexi. He's an adventurous rascal. I'm always finding him in the kitchen causing trouble."

"Adventurous, is he? He seems quite content with me. Shall I take him back to the temple? We could use a mouser in the temple garden to keep the mice away."

"Of course," replied Mayet. "I have three more of Ebony's kits to find homes for, but it should be easy. Everyone likes Ebony's kits.

"Do tell me about your studies at Karnak," Mayet continued.

Hotep grinned. "It's fascinating, especially the books by the great Imhotep. Which reminds me, Mother, I have a question to ask of you. How did you happen to name me *Hotep*, that is, *Imhotep*? One of the students said it was very bold of me to call myself Imhotep, as he was the most admired doctor in the history of Egypt."

Psssst!

Not everyone in Ancient Egypt could read or write. Those who could were called "scribes," and studied hieroglyphics and *hieratics* for many years under the guidance of the priests in temples. The temple at Karnak was known for its books of medical knowledge.

"That is true. Your great-grandfather's brother was called Imhotep, but he did not become a doctor. Imhotep seems to be a family name. But your father is a doctor and works for the military. He claims his family descended from the great Imhotep, and he hopes that you too will become a doctor."

"That is my wish, too, Mother. I will explain this to her."

"Her?" Mayet asked.

Hotep's ears reddened. "Yes, her name is Hygenia, and she wishes to become a doctor, too."

"Good!" said Mayet firmly. "We need more lady doctors."

I looked forward to meeting the lady doctor who made Hotep's ears turn pink!

And so it was that after the holiday I went with Hotep to Karnak, where students first became scribes, and then continued to learn their chosen vocation, whether as doctors, priests, architects, builders, government managers, or other positions that required the ability to read and write.

What a view of the world!

Chapter Two

Sharp Fangs and a Lisp

My favourite perch was on Hotep's shoulder. What a view of the world! Hotep and his mother had made a shoulder pad, with straps that crossed to his waist. This extra piece of linen was thick, allowing me to hold on when Hotep moved without hurting him.

Hotep became so accustomed to my sitting on his shoulder that when his visit was over and he went back to school, I went, too.

Mama Ebony gave me a proper bath before I left and told me about my father, Alexander Catt the First, who was also an adventurous feline. I was named after him, but Mama said he was known as "Alex." "Lexi" suits me just fine.

I said goodbye to Mama, hopped onto Hotep's shoulder and away we went.

Hotep's school was in a huge temple complex in Karnak. He walked to the Nile River and we boarded a river taxi to go downstream to Karnak. When we arrived, he walked up the hill. The temple was beautiful and seemed to grow bigger as we came nearer. The columns of the temple made Hotep seem like the dwarf god Bes. I felt as tiny as a mere kit compared with a mighty lion.

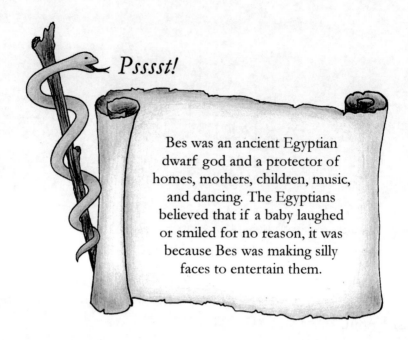

Psssst!

Bes was an ancient Egyptian dwarf god and a protector of homes, mothers, children, music, and dancing. The Egyptians believed that if a baby laughed or smiled for no reason, it was because Bes was making silly faces to entertain them.

Hotep was respected by the other students, but they teased him about his shoulder harness and me.

"The 'Gentle Giant' needs a feline bodyguard?" laughed one young fellow.

Hotep just smiled and said, "His name is Lexi and he will bring me luck because he is one of Bastet's kin."

The students came one by one to give me a stroke for luck.

One student was a beautiful young lady. "Hello, Mau mau. My name is Hygenia. My friends call me Genie," she said, gently patting me on the head and looking into my eyes. I blinked; Genie blinked back. I liked her, so I purred. Then I felt a trembling earthquake coming from my perch.

Genie smiled at Hotep. "Aaaww! He's purring! You have a beautiful cat."

"Yes, thank you," croaked Hotep nervously. "His name is Lexi."

"Nice name. I'm sure he will serve you well." Genie moved away and the "earthquake" from Hotep faded.

When Hotep's class began, I found out that they were studying medicines. Part of their learning took place in the garden of herbs next to the temple. The students tended this garden with great care. When Hotep kneeled to weed the plants, I hopped down and walked around smelling the herbs because I was curious.

The plants' leaves tickled my tail. At first, it was pleasant; but then it wasn't. I moved into a clear space, but my tail began to twitch, and it hurt. What did it mean?

Genie's voice rose in agitation, "No, no, no! You're removing the radishes—not the weeds!" She was scolding Hotep. His ears were bright red with embarrassment.

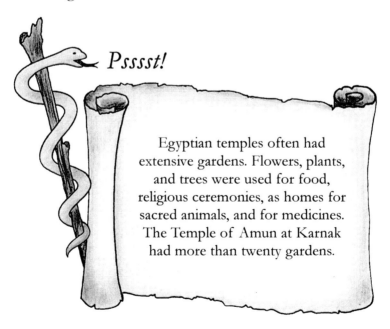

Psssst!

Egyptian temples often had extensive gardens. Flowers, plants, and trees were used for food, religious ceremonies, as homes for sacred animals, and for medicines. The Temple of Amun at Karnak had more than twenty gardens.

Lexi meets Khleo.

I looked around to see if anyone else had noticed, hoping Hotep would not be teased about this mistake. *Was this why my tail was twitching?* Then I saw a pair of eyes, watching me through the parsley leaves.

"Hello, Lessssi!" greeted a slithery female voice.

I couldn't see a body. Who was this creature that knew who I was?

"Come out and show me who you are. And my name is Lexi!" I corrected her. "Short for Alexander Catt II," I added proudly.

"Yessss, Lessssi. That wassss what I ssssaid. Sssso don't be rude. My name issss Khleo." She began to come through the parsley. She was a small snake. I flattened my ears and backed up.

Mama had taught me that cats in Egypt kill snakes, but I saw that she was an asp, and that meant she was poisonous.

What should I do?

Pssssst!

Several kinds of poisonous snakes that lived in the Nile region of ancient Egypt were called asps. Asps were a symbol of royalty and protection; crowns and armbands were often shaped like snakes, and even made of gold. Today, these snakes are called Egyptian cobras.

"Ssss! Ssss! Ssss!" she laughed. "Khleo for short or long! Can you ssssay my name, or hassss the cat got your tongue? Ssss, ssss, ssss!" she laughed again.

Then seeing that I was scared of her, she took advantage.

Before I could move a muscle, she circled and lunged at me with her mouth wide open, so I was looking right down her throat! She dropped just as suddenly and slithered between my legs to Genie.

She moved as fast as an ibis hunting fish.

For a small snake she had remarkably long, sharp fangs and a sharper tongue! I was speechless.

"Oh, look! Lexi has met Khleo!" cried Genie. She extended her arm to Khleo who wrapped herself around it like a bracelet.

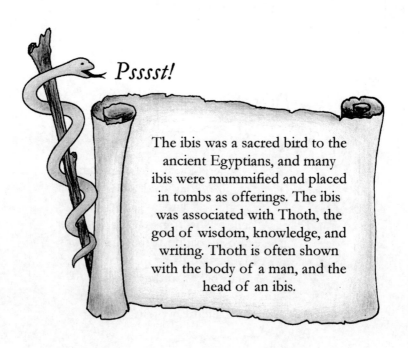

Pssst!

The ibis was a sacred bird to the ancient Egyptians, and many ibis were mummified and placed in tombs as offerings. The ibis was associated with Thoth, the god of wisdom, knowledge, and writing. Thoth is often shown with the body of a man, and the head of an ibis.

Genie continued to explain leaf shapes to Hotep in a soft voice. Khleo added esses whenever she wanted. I climbed up onto Hotep's shoulder and looked down on the little serpent. Hotep didn't order me to kill her; she seemed to be Genie's pet.

Genie helped replant the radishes and remove the bad weeds. When they finished, Hotep helped Genie collect some herbs for the temple clinic. Hotep's ears were still pink!

Khleo had vanished from Genie's arm and was now circling her hair, which was tied up at the back. Her hair looked a little like a donkey's tail. I mewed nervously.

Hotep patted me and explained, "Khleo is Genie's pet asp. Genie has removed the little asp's poison sacks. So don't worry, little friend, she can't kill you."

Well, that was a relief, but she could still bite me and that tongue could rip a cat's heart out. *Meow*! I promised myself to keep my kitty wits as sharp as Khleo's fangs!

My tail told me this was serious.

Chapter Three

Medicines and Mischief

The next morning, freshly scrubbed, all the students attended their classes at the House of Life. When their classes were finished, they continued on to the temple's clinic, called the House of Healing, to work with the patients of the day.

Lufaa, a priest of the temple, supervised and received the offerings to the gods from the patients. Vegetables, a bag of natron salt, a sack of quails, a bolt of linen, baskets of dates, jewellery, bread, and even a pig were graciously accepted and stored.

The line of people went on and on. So I padded outside to see how many patients were still waiting with offerings. It was then that my tail began to twitch, again. It was very uncomfortable.

I wandered down the line of waiting patients. A mother held her child in her arms. He was pale and had two red spots on his cheeks. He stirred restlessly and whimpered.

Further on I saw a boy lying on a litter bleeding and moaning. My tail told me it was serious. So I meowed loudly at the women ahead. After some persistent noise they turned to look at the noisy cat and, seeing the boy bleeding, they allowed the men holding the litter to pass ahead in the line. A young woman, who looked like his sister, carried his payment offering and followed me.

Psssst!

There was no money in ancient Egypt. All goods and services were traded, and people were paid for their labour in food, jewellery, or material goods. These gifts enabled the temples to continue their operations and services.

Hotep knew exactly what to do when he saw the gashed leg. He heated his instruments and stopped the flow of blood. He cleaned the wound with an ointment mixture of ibis fat, fir oil, and crushed peas. Then he spread honey on the wound to prevent infection, and stitched it up with a copper needle and linen thread. The injured young man awoke from a faint and thanked Hotep, praising him as "a true priest of Sekhmet." That meant "surgeon."

When Hotep started treating scorpion stings, which was an everyday, routine problem, I wandered off to find Genie. I found her in a room of statues.

Genie sat on a low stool beside a pregnant lady lying on a couch by the wall.

It wasn't a mouse tail!

Genie's medicine cabinet was nearby. I spotted a tail sticking out from under the cabinet. It moved back and forth, back and forth, as if it were wagging, but it wasn't a dog's tail. It looked more like a mouse's! A mouse! What was I thinking? Imhotep brought me to catch the mice.

I ran over and pounced. I had the tail pinned to the ground. It wiggled a bit and then stopped. I pulled and pulled. It was a long tail, and it didn't belong to a mouse!

"Are you ssssearching for ssssomething, Lessssi?" asked a familiar voice in my ear.

I looked at the thing I'd pulled out. It was Khleo's skin! Was she naked?

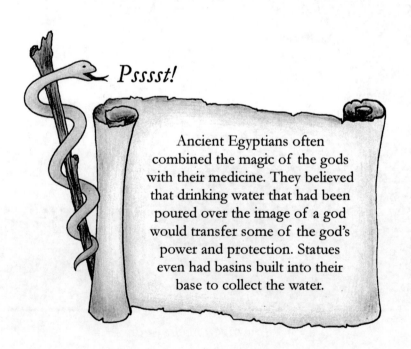

Pssssst!

Ancient Egyptians often combined the magic of the gods with their medicine. They believed that drinking water that had been poured over the image of a god would transfer some of the god's power and protection. Statues even had basins built into their base to collect the water.

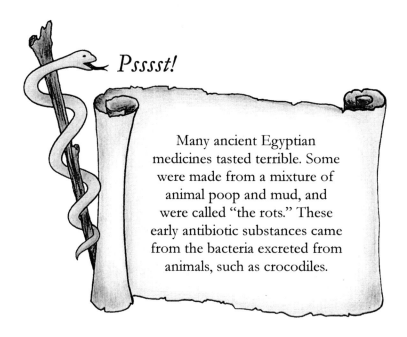

Psssst!

Many ancient Egyptian medicines tasted terrible. Some were made from a mixture of animal poop and mud, and were called "the rots." These early antibiotic substances came from the bacteria excreted from animals, such as crocodiles.

I turned my head and stared into snake eyes. Khleo dangled down from the cabinet. She had a new coat and looked very shiny.

I pulled back gingerly, cautiously, and bumped into Genie.

Genie said, "Not now, Lexi, you'll make me spill the water! Stay out of the way, I'm busy."

Khleo laughed, "Ssss, ssss, ssss!"

Genie poured some water over a statue of Hathor, the goddess who protected pregnant women. She carefully collected the water and urged the lady to drink the whole cup.

"This will give you the goddess's protection," said Genie. "Come and see me next week." The woman looked calm and happy as she left.

Genie's next patient was the whimpering, feverish boy.

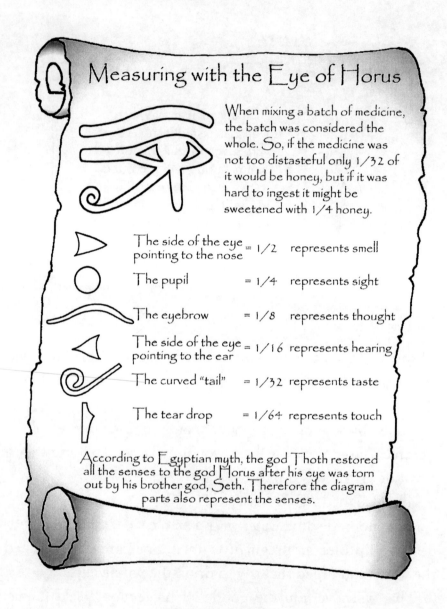

Measuring with the Eye of Horus

When mixing a batch of medicine, the batch was considered the whole. So, if the medicine was not too distasteful only 1/32 of it would be honey, but if it was hard to ingest it might be sweetened with 1/4 honey.

The side of the eye pointing to the nose = 1/2 represents smell

The pupil = 1/4 represents sight

The eyebrow = 1/8 represents thought

The side of the eye pointing to the ear = 1/16 represents hearing

The curved "tail" = 1/32 represents taste

The tear drop = 1/64 represents touch

According to Egyptian myth, the god Thoth restored all the senses to the god Horus after his eye was torn out by his brother god, Seth. Therefore the diagram parts also represent the senses.

The Eye of Horus

Genie's gentle hands quickly examined him. "River Fever," said Genie to the mother. "There's an outbreak every year."

The mother stroked his hair. "Can you do something? He's so sick!"

"Yes, right away," assured Genie and she searched her medicine cabinet. "Oh dear, this is the last of it. I'll use this and then make some more. Come back tomorrow and I'll have a new supply for his next dose."

She offered the boy a little cup of the medicine. It must have tasted horrible because it took a long time for both doctor and mother to persuade the little boy to drink it. I sniffed the empty cup after and it certainly smelled foul.

When the clinic closed, Genie hired an errand boy. "Go down to the river and collect crocodile dung. You know the place. Here is the jar."

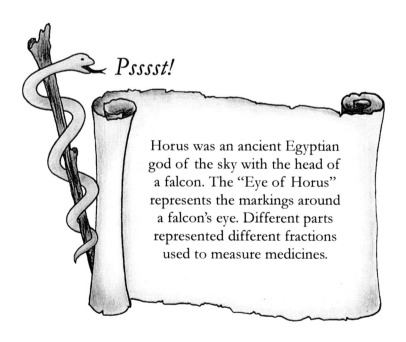

Pssssst!

Horus was an ancient Egyptian god of the sky with the head of a falcon. The "Eye of Horus" represents the markings around a falcon's eye. Different parts represented different fractions used to measure medicines.

Playing a trick on Khleo

"Yes, Doctor, I've collected it many times for the clinic. I'll be back really fast!"

Croc poop! That was the smell! Icky! The little boy had good reason to refuse to swallow his medicine.

Then I had an idea! Maybe this could be a way to play a trick on Khleo for all her teasing!

That night I watched Genie grinding herbs by lamplight. Using the Eye of Horus as a guide, Genie measured the ground herbs carefully and wrote the prescription on the top of the pill jar. It looked like a series of plant drawings followed by the part of the Eye of Horus that showed the dose followed by the herb's name.

As Genie put each ingredient in a bowl, Khleo stirred the mixture with her tail until all was combined. When Genie said, "That's enough," Khleo lowered her head and shook her tail vigorously. Herbs flew around. I leapt aside; I didn't fancy licking that mess off my fur.

"Ssssscaredy cat!" scoffed Khleo and flicked one more wad of herbs at me. Teeth, tongue, and tail, Khleo was a whole package of trouble looking for me.

At the top of the box, Genie drew a big "Rx" with a long tail. This labelled the work as her prescription. She put her name at the end and added the letters "swnt," which meant she was a lady doctor. Genie was an excellent doctor of herbs.

She cleaned her hands and left the medicine room.

I spotted another jar—the large jar of crocodile poop!

It was time to play a trick on Khleo.

I pussyfooted over to the empty jars. It wasn't difficult to identify the freshly collected, pungent crocodile dung. Luckily, the jar had a wide mouth and wasn't too tall. I placed my front paws on the lip of the jar and carefully flattened my ears and tucked my head into the jar. The smell was foul, but I made smacking sounds that echoed inside the jar. I twitched my tail, emerged from the jar, and licked my kitty muzzle with great enthusiasm. I sniffed the jar again and grinned as if I was having the time of my life. Once more, I briefly tucked my head inside the jar and made a huge slurping sound. I retreated and, licking my muzzle again, I slowly left the room.

At the archway, I glanced back over my shoulder. As I expected, Khleo couldn't wait to see what I thought was so delicious. She had slithered over the table and up over the other jars to taste the kitty treat for herself. Excitement and speed overcame caution and Khleo fell into the jar of dung. Served her right!

I passed Genie, returning to the medicine room. A moment later, Genie was scolding Khleo. "Stay out of these medicine jars when I'm not here. If you eat some inappropriate herb, you could get sick, Khleo, and that's all I need—a sick snake!"

Genie grumbled as she wiped down her little snake, and then angrily threw Khleo into a basin of water to finish the job. Khleo swam vigorously around, and then slithered onto the table and shook off the water, hissing to herself like a mad cobra. "I'll get that tricksssster for being so nassssty!"

I returned to Hotep in the surgery annex, where the surgical instruments were kept. He was trying to see if thin slivers, cut from reeds, could be used for needles instead of using copper.

Hotep said, "Look Lexi! The reeds are strong enough and sharp—you know how sharp, don't you?"

"Meow!" I winced, remembering the reed splinter in my paw.

"Think of it, a disposable needle—use once; throw away. Is it not wonderful to live in this modern age of Ramses II?"

Meow! It certainly was and I was lucky to know these two young doctors: one to fix me up if I had an accident and one to prevent me from being ill. The only trouble was … one angry, smart-asp snake!

Welcome to Deir el-Medina.

CHAPTER FOUR

A TOWNFUL OF TROUBLE

Hotep and Genie had studied hard for a long time. They seemed to know the medical books at the House of Life by heart, and now consulted them very rarely.

One day, the Chief Physician-Priest Lufaa called them to his room.

"We have a special need for your talents, Hotep and Genie. The doctor at Deir el-Medina—Doctor Metu—is getting old. Soon the tomb workers will return from their labours in the fields, tired and injured. There will be too many of them for Doctor Metu to tend, especially for the unexpected cases. He needs two doctors to assist him, and you are both ready to serve. You will leave at the end of the week. Are there any questions?"

"Yes," answered Hotep and turned to Genie. "Shall we divide the work? I could do all the surgery and help you mix your medicines."

"Yes. We can sort the cases in the morning. I will tend the sick, prescribe the medicines, and we can both work to improve the health of the community," answered Genie.

In three days, they were packed and they didn't forget to take me! Or Khleo!

Deir el-Medina was not far from Karnak, almost directly across the Nile, with an hour's uphill walk from the river bank.

Psssst!

Deir el-Medina was a village in ancient Egypt, located two miles from the West Bank of the Nile at Thebes. The stonecutters, sculptors, carpenters, painters, potters, and other workmen who built and decorated the tombs in the Valley of the Kings lived in Deir el-Medina.

The community served the workers who carved out the tombs in the Valley of the Kings.

I had imagined a small work camp, with patients requiring care for banged fingers, colds, upset stomachs, and of course scorpion stings. I thought it would be a piece of honey cake! Sweet and small—giving the three of us time for adventure in the Valley of the Kings. Was I ever wrong! When its workers were in full force, Deir el-Medina was chaotic and loaded with trouble!

The two-mile walk uphill in the desert heat was hard for Genie who was rather small, but of course easy for Hotep who just loped along on his long legs. Their baskets of instruments, bandages, medicines, and personal belongings were carried by local youths hired on the Nile's west shore.

When Deir el-Medina came into sight, I realized it was much larger than I'd expected. My tail didn't twitch, but it began to ache—a new and horrid sensation.

Then, when we approached the village, I could smell trouble. Not the exciting scruff-of-the-neck trouble, but a rotten, stinky, real, and repulsive trouble.

Hotep and Genie stopped as soon as they'd entered the village, and looked and listened. Besides the nasty odour, babies were crying, people were yelling at each other, and several crashes and bangs warned us this was not a happy place.

An older man in a white robe was making his way down the steps of the town, leaning heavily on his cane. He shooed away two women and a dog, and approached us with a big smile on his face.

"Doctor Imhotep? Doctor Hygenia? Is it really you, at last? I have been writing that old croc of a priest for a year. He said you weren't ready. I said I'd train you. He said you needed to study the texts. 'Let them learn on the job,' I said."

Genie stopped this flow of words by extending her hand and saying, "Call me Genie."

"My girl, you are as pretty as a lotus! You can call me Metu."

"And I am Hotep, named after Imhotep, the great vizier doctor and pray I am worthy of the honour."

"My boy, you are certain to be, I'm sure." Metu looked up and down Hotep's frame. "I hope your bed is long enough.

"You brought a cat! We need cats in the Deir. I hope he's a good mouser."

The venerable doctor was evidently too deaf to hear the hisses coming from Genie's bag.

"Come," he said, "I'll show you to your rooms. But I warn you, I haven't had time to get them cleaned."

Cleaning house

Our living quarters were dirty, just as we'd been warned. Genie asked for Metu's servants' help, and soon after, one lady appeared. Genie promised more beer and figs to the young men who had carried our baskets, and they eagerly started cleaning. Hotep located fleabane in the carryalls and started fumigating. I chased out a couple of rats. Khleo did nothing but hiss her displeasure! Useless snake!

By the time the sun was low in the West, our home was clean and orderly. Incense burned on the fire. Doctor Metu sent an invitation for supper.

"Good, I won't have to cook. It has been a long day," said Genie. "And it'll be an excellent opportunity to start organizing what must be done for the town."

Doctor Metu talked all through dinner. *Did he ever stop talking?* I wondered. However, there were several important points he made clear.

First, the whole town was filthy. The labourers had left their homes in Deir el-Medina to farm their fields along the Nile. But they would soon return to work on Ramses' tomb and the tomb for his children, which had space for almost a hundred bodies. Only those people who worked for the town were presently living in the town.

Second, a disease had broken out in the lower east side of the town, and Doctor Metu couldn't identify it. He was worried. He wanted to know what it was and what to do about it before the workers returned.

And third, rats overran every house.

"We need more cats!" said Doctor Metu.

Lexi ousts the rats.

CHAPTER FIVE

COMMUNITY CLEANUP

The next morning Doctor Metu opened the House of Healing and, with three doctors, the work of tending to scorpion bites, eye infections, and small cuts was done in an hour.

Hotep asked Doctor Metu to show him the granaries, while Genie set out for the east side of the town. This time, I followed Genie because I wanted to see the town.

"Doctor! Doctor!" called a lady from a rundown house. "My child is so sick. What can I do?" Khleo hid herself in Genie's bag. The little snake had no patience with children.

"Show me," ordered Genie as we entered the house. Genie examined the child. She placed her hands on the child's head to check for fever, and then on his hands to count the blood pulses. I investigated the yard kitchen and caught and killed a small rat. Their grain jar was leaking grain and needed repair. No wonder there were rats.

It was not surprising Hotep had gone to check the town's grain supply first. Cutting down the rats' food supply would cut down the rat problem.

Genie instructed the child's mother how to reduce the fever. She gave her fleabane for the house and medicine for the child.

I wondered if it had crocodile dung in it?

"You will have fewer problems if you clean your house, I promise you," said Genie. "Drink red wine with honey, often, along with a small amount of yeast. Then you will feel better, too."

Genie and I visited fifteen homes that afternoon. We were both tired when we climbed the hill through the town.

Hotep looked questioningly at Genie upon our return.

"Smallpox," she said.

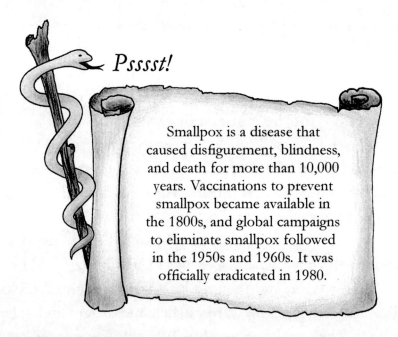

Psssst!

Smallpox is a disease that caused disfigurement, blindness, and death for more than 10,000 years. Vaccinations to prevent smallpox became available in the 1800s, and global campaigns to eliminate smallpox followed in the 1950s and 1960s. It was officially eradicated in 1980.

For weeks, the three doctors went from house to house. At first, the smallpox kept spreading and then the spread eased. People helped each other. Granary jars were repaired. Rodent holes were blocked. Fleabane was spread.

One persistently crying baby stopped crying instantly with another of Genie's foul-smelling remedies. The child wasn't sick, just cranky, I guess. *Meow!* I was glad I wasn't cranky!

Word came that most of the crops grown along the river bank had been collected and stored. The workers and their families would soon return. Meanwhile, Hotep recruited as many free hands as he could, and they cleaned the empty houses and drove out the vermin. A few talented people painted murals on the walls. Other walls were freshly whitewashed. Meanwhile, the House of Healing was open every morning.

Then the workers arrived—a trickle at first—and once more life changed. Sennudjem, the foreman, came first, bringing supplies of food, tools, and materials to finish the tombs. He brought a few cats, too, and they helped with the rat problem.

Time passed as fast as Osiris's chariot. The workers set to task on the tomb for Ramses' children with great enthusiasm, relieved that they didn't have to clean their houses first. There were no new cases of smallpox.

And then disaster struck!

Disaster strikes!

Chapter Six

The Rescue

The House of Healing was in full operation that morning, and Genie and I were inspecting the line-up. I had just passed a crying child, thinking *I know what you're going to get!* when my tail gave me a sharp, sudden pain.

I spun around, thinking the child had stepped on it! But there was no one near me. Then everyone, including me, felt a tremble.

"Earthquake!" someone shouted.

Khleo dropped from Genie's hair and had a hissy fit on the ground. Baah! Hysterical hisser!

It might have started as an earthquake, but as we looked around, we saw a cloud of dust rising from the tombs. Genie and Hotep grabbed medicines and supplies for injuries. Husky men in the village carried the medical supplies and some litters. The three doctors set out at a brisk pace, Metu leading the way. Even with his cane, he was amazingly fast and knew the easiest route.

Genie carried her staff to help her walk on the uneven ground. Khleo wrapped herself around it near the top, which gave her a better view than I had. She hissed an alarm.

We neared the construction site, and were dismayed by the huge cloud of dust hovering over it.

Perched on Hotep's shoulder, I saw runners coming toward us.

"There was a weakness in the mountain where we were preparing burial chambers for Pharaoh Ramses' family. The walls collapsed. Many men are trapped. Maybe some are killed, we do not know."

"I will help with the rescue," volunteered Hotep.

"I will sort the injured," said Metu, "into three groups: those we attend immediately; those who can wait; and those who are beyond help."

"And I will clean and attend the wounds," said Genie. Khleo still hissed in alarm. Useless reptile! Sometimes I wished Genie would leave her at home.

One of the muscular men hoisted Doctor Metu onto his back and we made record time along the path to the site. Dust continued to pour from the opening as the workers dug to save men.

Hotep rushed into the tomb. I was still on his shoulder and started coughing from the dust before he did.

In the gloom, two men supported another man with a broken leg. I hoped Genie had enough reeds for splints. The ceiling lowered and Hotep stooped and then lowered himself to his hands and knees.

There was no way I could help, so I began following the dust moving toward the mouth of the tomb.

A puff of dust led me into a wrong turn. My cat's eyes could see well enough to know we hadn't come in this way. I figured

The Rescue

the dusty puff should have been going away from me toward the entrance—not coming at me—so I turned around.

Then I heard a scraping sound. A rat? I stopped to listen and, with my heart pounding in excitement, I guessed this was someone trying to get out of trouble!

A feeble, "Help," came from the wall.

I scampered up the passage to the corner where I'd turned in error. I yowled as loudly as I possibly could. Several workers passed me, hurrying to rescue others deeper in the tunnel. I kept yowling as hard as I could. I could hear voices in the deep tunnel echoing in the gloom.

"A cat! Are you sure?" It was Hotep's voice. He was beside me in moments and had another worker with him.

"Show me, Lexi!" Hotep ordered, so I led him down the side tunnel, stopping by the spot where I'd heard the scraping sound. I meowed urgently.

"Help!" came a faint voice.

Hotep and the worker dug into the rubble. The dust was awful, but I waited for the rescue. Carefully, Hotep pulled out a young man. He had a broken arm and a bad gash on his shaven head.

"How did you know where I was?" asked the young man.

"Lexi, my cat, told us," Hotep said as he carried the man up the main corridor. As soon as I was free of the tomb's entrance, I shook myself like a dog. The fresh air smelled so sweet!

Hotep put the young man down near Genie who set to work. First, she stopped the flow of blood from his head wound. She knew that head wounds always bleed a lot and often look worse than they are. She covered it with linen tape. Then she attended to his broken arm with gentle fingers, finding the break.

He looked earnestly at her and said clearly, "Tell Amen I'm sorry!" and then he passed out as she straightened his arm and set it with splints.

I mewed in sympathy but wondered, *Who is Amen?*

As the story of my rescuing the worker circulated, everyone wanted to give a pat to the lucky cat.

"Maybe we should always have a cat in the tombs," said one man as he patted me so hard more dust puffed out of my fur. I shook myself again and started to bathe, but Genie brushed me vigorously with a linen cloth.

"It wouldn't be good for your tummy to lick too much dust, Lexi!"

Dusty hairballs! I agreed. I couldn't get the taste out of my mouth! Genie gave me a drink of water and that helped.

I settled down beside a crying boy with a broken leg and he put his arm around me and whimpered. Genie gave him a drink of beer with a pinch of mandrake to help him fall asleep. Khleo fixed her tail in his hair and wiped his brow with a damp cloth while Genie cleaned the wound with oil of fir and set his leg with reeds. I guess Khleo wasn't entirely useless. Finally, Genie covered the broken skin with honey to prevent infection.

Someone told Genie the boy was called Amen, and that he was the construction crew's errand boy who brought them food and beer.

Triage

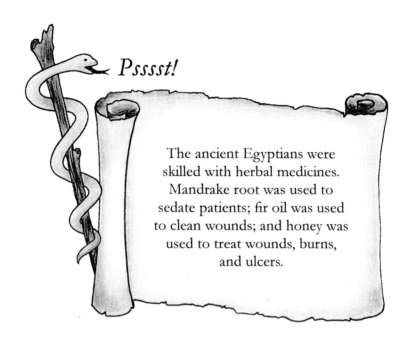

Psssst!

The ancient Egyptians were
skilled with herbal medicines.
Mandrake root was used to
sedate patients; fir oil was used
to clean wounds; and honey was
used to treat wounds, burns,
and ulcers.

All day the doctors worked. At last, all the workers were accounted for, and twenty-five wounded were carried down the hill on litters. As Genie and Hotep followed the last of the litters, Genie told Hotep what the young man had said. Genie wondered if Amen was the errand boy, and why the young man had said he was sorry. Hotep said he'd try to find out.

Back in town, Doctor Metu's staff had gathered some cooks, and soup and fresh bread were soon ready outside the House of Healing. Hotep poured some soup into a small bowl for me. Nothing had ever tasted so good.

Sennudjem, the foreman, checked the workers gathered for the food, including the injured. He reported to Genie and Hotep, "There's one missing. He signed his name as 'Ka' on my list. But that can't be right? He wasn't a spirit. Can you help me find him?"

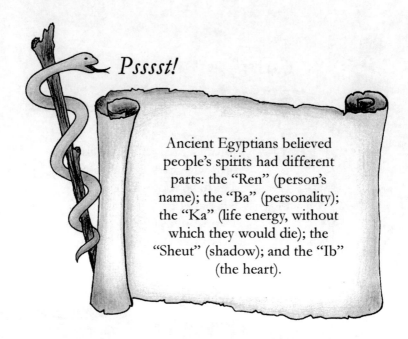

Psssst!

Ancient Egyptians believed
people's spirits had different
parts: the "Ren" (person's
name); the "Ba" (personality);
the "Ka" (life energy, without
which they would die); the
"Sheut" (shadow); and the "Ib"
(the heart).

Genie and Hotep looked for the injured young man among the wounded, but couldn't find him.

Hotep looked for the young man in the village, but no-one had seen him.

They checked the clinic line-ups in the following days, but he did not show up. It was evident that he had left Deir el-Medina still suffering from a broken arm.

Several months passed and more workers were needed to build the tombs. The village swelled to thousands of people. Many lived in tents. A larger water supply was needed for so many people, so a community reservoir was built and kept full by men trekking almost two miles to fresh water. People lined up morning and night to fill their household jugs.

One day a man brought a letter from the "croc-o-doc" at

Karnak. It was addressed to Hotep and Genie, and within its folds was a letter from the Pharaoh, who mentioned having an aching tooth; he summoned my favourite doc's to Heliopolis. I quickly learned that Heliopolis was the largest city in Egypt, and was far down the Nile River in Lower Egypt. The Pharaoh had heard the praises of Hotep and Genie, and wished to consult with them. He also ordered them to bring their cat, Lexi of Luxor. *Me!*

The Karnak croc-o-doc's letter held assurances that two other young doctors were on their way to the Deir to assist Doctor Metu.

It was late summer, and the Nile was still in flood. After a flurry of packing and tearful goodbyes, we began our little parade out of the village. The water carriers took charge of the baskets of provisions and belongings, and the villagers lined the streets waving and bearing gifts.

I was bursting with excitement. It would be our first long and adventurous trip, and I looked forward to seeing the big boat necessary for such an expedition that would take weeks. Would we have sails fluttering in the breeze? Would a hundred men pull on the oars? Would we see hippopotami and crocodiles?

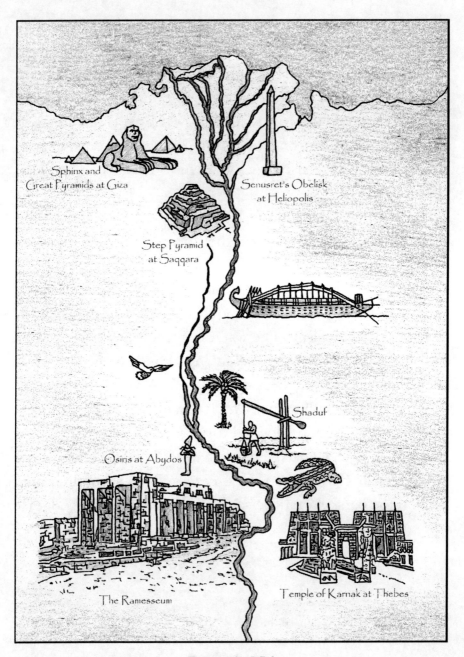

Down the Nile

CHAPTER SEVEN

DOWN THE NILE

We caught a small boat that ran a taxi service between the west shore and the docks at Thebes. There, we were directed to Pharaoh Ramses' beautiful *felucca*. It was freshly painted and clean, but there were no sails. The current of the Nile ran north, and carried large boats easily and quickly. The oars, however, were ready.

Genie and I looked at the fine view of Hatshepsut's temple to the west, and we could also see the progress of the Ramesseum being built.

Hotep chatted with the captain who was keeping an eye on the loading of his cargo, and the boarding of people like us travelling to the delta.

"Have you travelled farther south?" asked Hotep.

"All the way to Silsileh, but I don't recommend it," answered the captain.

"Why not?" asked Hotep.

"The sandbars of the river around the great bend are bad enough, but the river south is full of rocky cataracts. Boats easily capsize there, and the crocodiles love that. That is where the Temple of Sobek, the crocodile god, is located, you know."

"I've never seen a crocodile," said Hotep. "I've certainly seen enough of their poop! But never the actual croc. I guess they prefer to be under the water, out of sight."

"Believe me, you wouldn't want to see one, because if you did, it would be too late for you!" laughed the captain.

He gave a signal and the crew pushed off from the dock. We started moving right away, and soon turned to the east, to navigate "the crook" of the river.

The captain moved toward the prow to direct his crew through the tricky turns of the river, which we could soon see were full of sandbars.

We looked up at the fluttering red banners and painted pylons of the Temple of Karnak, and then stood at the side to watch the navigation and view the towns along the thirty-mile leg eastward. The captain often barked orders to the crew straining at the oars, and to the helmsman who managed the tiller.

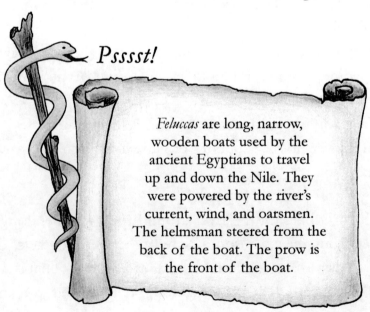

Pssssst!

Feluccas are long, narrow, wooden boats used by the ancient Egyptians to travel up and down the Nile. They were powered by the river's current, wind, and oarsmen. The helmsman steered from the back of the boat. The prow is the front of the boat.

As we turned north, there were more sandbars. Every passenger held their breath, listening to the grunting oarsmen who were pulling hard to avoid getting the felucca stuck in the sand. But they were too late.

The bottom of the boat rasped along the sand and the boat tipped! *Oh, Meow!* The sound was frightening.

Hotep and I looked over the edge at the sandbar. We had a full view of a crocodile rushing across the sand. He opened his mouth and bit one of the oars pushing against the sand. The oarsman screamed and pulled back his broken oar. The rest of the crew pushed their oars with a mighty effort. The boat shuddered as it broke free. The crew cheered! Once more, we moved quickly over the water.

I looked back at Genie holding onto the other side. She looked pale and frightened. Hotep didn't mention the crocodile, which she hadn't seen. As we turned west, back to the Nile's northern flow, the tension among the passengers and crew eased a bit, and we looked forward to our first stop and next meal.

While the captain of the felucca managed to navigate the crook of the Nile, Khleo stayed in her basket. Discomfort and danger always made her hide. But once we were in the broad, smooth flow of the river, she decided to take a sunbath. She laid herself out along the line of the deck's planks and sighed with contentment.

Hygenia, however, was distracted by the active *shadufs* lifting water to the precious crops. Imhotep was chatting with the helmsman at the tiller. I was the only one who had reason to watch the little snake.

The oarsman screamed!

Unexpectedly, the crewman with the broken oar rose to get another one. He spotted Khleo.

"A snake!" he shouted, and raised his oar to strike the little serpent.

It worked before, I thought to myself, so I leapt out and stabbed his bare foot with my claw. Just as fast, I hid behind Genie.

The crewman screamed, "I've been stung! A scorpion has stung me!"

Genie turned to see blood trickling down his foot, as Khleo slithered into her basket. Genie stooped to look at the man's wound, and said, "That's not a scorpion sting. It's bleeding."

She calmly pulled out a small piece of linen and pressed it to the wound. She looked at me with a suspicious glint in her pretty eyes.

I gave myself a bath. That activity always seems to help awkward situations regain their dignity and calm, and gives me the appearance of innocence.

The man continued with his errand when he saw no snake and no scorpion.

Genie returned to her interest in irrigation, and a quiet, muffled voice said, "Thank you, Lessssi. I owe you."

As the days passed, we saw the city of Abydos where Osiris was buried, and Assiut, a city green with date palms, sycamore and pomegranate trees, and flax and wheat fields.

Then the river narrowed, with cliffs on both sides. The cliffs were full of countless birds, fluttering and screaming as the gusts of wind pushed our boat toward more sand bars. The crew was busy again.

When we were through that treacherous stretch, we passed boats towing a large barge full of cut stone. Someone said it was for the Ramesseum. *Meow!* I wondered how it would get past the sand bars and the crocodiles!

It worked before …

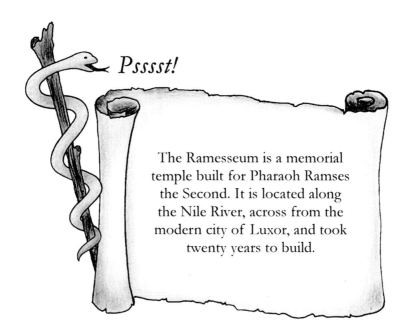

Psssst!

The Ramesseum is a memorial
temple built for Pharaoh Ramses
the Second. It is located along
the Nile River, across from the
modern city of Luxor, and took
twenty years to build.

After weeks of travel, we saw in the early morning light the Step
Pyramid at Saqqara. We hardly noticed the city of Memphis on
the eastern shore!

"Imagine," said Genie, "Imhotep built that marvellous pyramid! And he is your ancestor!"

"I wonder if I can live up to his name," said Hotep. "I'd like
to do something really important."

"You will," said Genie confidently.

Hotep's chin rose a fraction, and he took a deep breath. I
could almost hear his inner voice say, *I will.*

Meow! I echoed.

It wasn't long before the great pyramids of Giza came into
view and with them the great Sphinx.

Genie said, "The pyramids are impressive. They are larger than

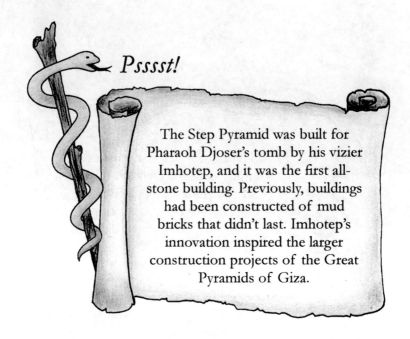

Psssst!

The Step Pyramid was built for Pharaoh Djoser's tomb by his vizier Imhotep, and it was the first all-stone building. Previously, buildings had been constructed of mud bricks that didn't last. Imhotep's innovation inspired the larger construction projects of the Great Pyramids of Giza.

I imagined. I've always dreamed of seeing Pharaoh Khafre's Sphinx. I can see he was a handsome king, wasn't he? But I wonder why he chose to have the body of a lion?"

"Meow!" I said.

Genie looked at me. "Sorry, Lexi. Of course that makes sense to choose the lion—the most proud and powerful of all the cats."

Satisfied, I looked at the sphinx again. I could tell by his big, straight nose and his proudly held head that he was a cat all the way through. The Sphinx was known to answer mysteries. I wondered if I posed like the big cat, could I solve mysteries too? *Meow!*

We were finally in Lower Egypt—the Delta—where the Nile split into many forks. It was obvious at once that this was very fertile land, as we saw lush gardens, vineyards, and grazing pastures.

We took the first branch to the east, and were soon in sight of Heliopolis and the Pharaoh's palace.

The docks were noisy with excitement. Part of the noise came from the braying donkeys waiting to transport people and goods. Pharaoh Ramses had provided several donkeys for us and our baskets. Hotep wished to walk, but he insisted that Genie ride. Hotep wanted me to ride with Genie, but Khleo was wrapped around her hair again; I dug my claws into Hotep's shoulder pad instead. I didn't dare risk a bite from Khleo's sharp fangs.

Soon our small parade moved on into the city. Heliopolis was clean and colourful. The houses sparkled with whitewash, shadowed with shapely trees.

The donkeys took us to the Pharaoh's stone palace where we were escorted to rooms filled with plush cushions, bowls of figs, and vases of lotus blossoms. From the verandah, we had a beautiful view of the city aglow in the setting sun.

"All this luxury to attend a royal toothache?" questioned Genie.

"It makes me wonder what treatment we'd get if he broke his royal leg!" said Hotep.

Servants brought us supper along with an invitation to Pharaoh Ramses' court for the morning. The invitation included Lexi Catt of Luxor—*Meow!* That was amazing! And Khleo wasn't mentioned. *Yeow!*

I hardly slept: I was so excited. But I wondered what they expected a mere cat could do for a Pharaoh's toothache?

Genie needsssss her privasssssy!

CHAPTER EIGHT

PREPARATIONS TO MEET ROYALTY

Genie rose early the next morning. She finished unpacking and set up her toilette. I watched as she set out her bronze razor, tweezers, and flaxseed oil soap. Separately she arranged the black Kohl and green malachite for her eyes. I knew that Egyptians used these cosmetics to protect their eyes from disease.

She also unpacked the wig that she used for formal occasions. There would not be any donkey's tail to hide Khleo today!

Khleo wove in and around the delicate display darting her tongue to smell the ingredients and softly hissing her approval. She slithered to the edge of the table and hissed at me.

"Lessssi! Have a little resssspect! Didn't your Mama Cat teach you your mannersssss? Have ssssome dessssenssssy. Genie needssss her privassssy!" Khleo hissed and lunged as if to bite me. I backed away carefully.

Genie scolded Khleo. "You rude little serpent! Didn't your mama teach you some manners? Stop hissing at Lexi. Show him a little respect. He's done nothing to you!" And she put Khleo in her basket and closed the lid.

Tail and nose high, I left with great dignity and went to Hotep's room. He was singing as he bathed. I gave myself a bath and I didn't care who was looking!

The Pharaoh's highest regard.

CHAPTER NINE

LEXI SOLVES THE MYSTERY

The Pharaoh's smile that morning was such a broad grin that I knew at once he didn't have a toothache.

The Great Hall where the Pharaoh held his court was so enormous that several feluccas could have fitted inside it—with their sails up!

As instructed, we walked up the middle aisle. The crowd rose, stamped their feet, and cheered until we reached the throne.

People of authority and nobility surrounded the king. Next to him sat his beautiful royal wife, Nefertari.

Hotep and Genie bowed to Pharaoh Ramses. I bowed to the statue of Bastet that was next to the throne. I looked up to see Pharaoh Ramses smiling at me. I sat quietly and looked as poised and respectful as if I were a seated sphinx!

The Pharaoh rose to his feet, nodded first to Genie and then to Hotep. He was as tall as Hotep—even taller with the Double Crown of Egypt above his long narrow face. His hooked nose and strong chin showed his strength of character.

He grinned and announced, "I do not have a toothache."

He laughed and the whole room laughed with him.

"It was an excuse to tear you away from Deir el-Medina."

More foot stomping and cheering from the audience.

Pharaoh Ramses lifted his hand. All was quiet.

"Hotep, full name Imhotep, you have proven you are worthy of the name of our ancestral vizier and doctor. For cleaning a town of vermin; overseeing its restoration; acting as doctor of Sekhmet; and heroically rescuing twenty-five people from the collapse of the tomb, I hereby award you the medal of Imhotep. It gives you the Pharaoh's authority to improve the health and safety of the people of Egypt, and the authority to improve the health environment of the towns they live in. Wear it to show everyone in Egypt that the Pharaoh holds you in his highest regard."

Amidst a roar of approval, Pharaoh Ramses placed a huge gold medallion on a leather strap over Hotep's bowed head. Hotep raised his head and straightened. It looked like he'd grown another inch!

The Pharaoh raised his hand. Once more all was quiet.

"Genie, full name Hygenia. You are the clear descendant of Peseshet, the famous lady director of lady doctors. For defeating an outbreak of smallpox with outstanding ability in mixing medications; for teaching the benefits of cleanliness; and most of all for promoting the preventative measures that keep my people healthy and free of disease, I award you the medal of Lady-doctor Peseshet. This medal gives you the authority of the Pharaoh to improve the health and safety of the people of Egypt and to improve the health environment in which they live. Wear it to show everyone in Egypt that the Pharaoh holds you in his highest regard."

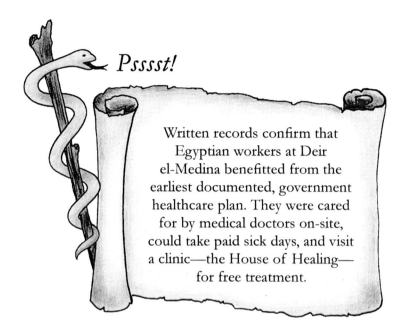

Psssst!

Written records confirm that Egyptian workers at Deir el-Medina benefitted from the earliest documented, government healthcare plan. They were cared for by medical doctors on-site, could take paid sick days, and visit a clinic—the House of Healing—for free treatment.

Another outburst of cheering swelled as the Pharaoh placed Genie's gold medallion over her head.

The noise continued for a while until the Pharaoh raised his hand. Then it ceased.

Pharaoh Ramses turned to watch me as I rubbed against a young man's leg and purred. The room was so quiet that my purring echoed around the hall.

The Pharaoh narrowed his eyes suspiciously. "How is it that Lexi knows my son, Pre-hir-wonmef?" he asked Hotep.

Hotep studied the young man's face and said, "When I saw him last he wore no hair, and he had a head wound and a broken arm. He is the man we rescued from the second cave-in in the tomb, but we did not know who he was. Lexi found him buried in some rubble, and yowled until we came to the rescue."

"I see," said the Pharaoh. "Pre-hir-wonmef, come before me!"

Pre-hir-wonmef walked forward with his head held high, but he was trembling. "Yes, Father," he said quietly.

Pharaoh Ramses studied his son for a moment and as he did I took my place beside his son. The Pharaoh glanced down at me and then asked, "Prehir, are you afraid of the demon, Ammut?"

I felt a shudder run through Pre-hir-wonmef as he whispered, "Yes, Father, a fear like no other."

"Then to save yourself, tell me the truth, according to Maat. Why were you in the tomb like a worker, and what do you know about the collapse of the tomb?"

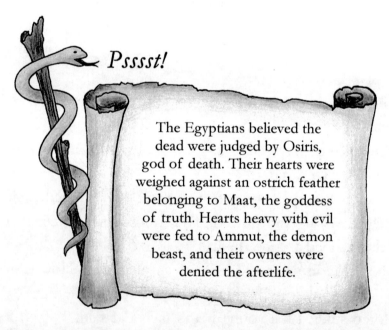

Pssst!

The Egyptians believed the dead were judged by Osiris, god of death. Their hearts were weighed against an ostrich feather belonging to Maat, the goddess of truth. Hearts heavy with evil were fed to Ammut, the demon beast, and their owners were denied the afterlife.

Prehir looked down at me. He bent down and patted my head, probably for luck. Then he looked his father in the eyes and said, "It all began with my brother, Amen-hir-khopshef. You always liked him best."

64

Osiris's judgement—the weighing of the heart

The Pharaoh frowned and twisted his head in puzzlement.

"And when we went to Kadesh," Prehir continued, "you made it clear that you trusted him more than me. You trusted him to fight with you in battle and protect your back. But you commanded me to go to safety with the women and children. I was humiliated. Then, when you designed the tomb, you gave Amen the central burial room and dedicated a special hall to him as well. It was too much. It hurt. I sabotaged both and was caught in my own jealous destruction. I am sorry. I immediately returned to Heliopolis to tell Amen how sorry I was."

Pharaoh Ramses turned to his son, Amen-hir-khopshef. "You knew?" he asked.

Amen stepped forward and put a hand on Prehir's shoulder. "Yes, Father. I do forgive Prehir, and I understand how he could feel jealous. I was proud that you chose me to protect you in the battle of Kadesh."

Pharaoh Ramses said, "I understand now, but I must explain to both of you. I value both of you equally, but for different reasons. You, Amen, are the eldest of all my sons and have more experience in battle. So it was a clear choice to order you to fight with me in the battle of Kadesh for the safety of the King of Egypt. However, the future of Egypt lies with my family. If I should perish, the new Pharaoh will be one of my sons, guided by his mother. Thus, I needed someone I trusted with the future of my country, and someone I knew could truly take care of my family. That was you, Prehir. That is my truth according to Maat. I am not going to judge you, Prehir. That is the duty of Osiris."

The Pharaoh's vizier, Paser, stepped forward and brought

Sennudjem, the foreman of the construction site with him. They bowed politely to the king.

"Oh, great Pharaoh," said Paser. "Sennudjem and I have examined the tomb carefully, and we are certain that the main damage was caused by Geb, god of the earth. His laughter made the earth quake. Your son was merely trying to scrape off tributes and names, which are easily repaired. Your son is fortunate that this feline heard his cry for help and drew attention to him."

"I see," the Pharaoh continued. "It is clear that I owe Lexi Catt for the life and trust of my son. Bastet surely smiles on you, Lexi.

"Alexander Catt II, known as Lexi of Luxor, for all of your excellent work as the chief mouse-catcher of Deir el-Medina, and for your heroic rescue of my son, I hereby award you the Ankh of Long Life."

He placed around my neck a small gold ankh, threaded on a thin black strap that disappeared into my fur so that just the medal twinkled on my breast. As he did this he said, "I knew your father, Alexander Catt the First. I see you are very much like him. Do you have any special feline request?"

I looked at Khleo, who was curled around Genie's wrist. Could the Pharaoh take her away from Genie? But I knew that would disappoint Genie too much. Could the Pharaoh punish Khleo? But that wouldn't be fair. I had played naughty pranks on her, too. So I shook my head, "No!" and I let bygones be bygones.

Lexi's award—the Ankh of Long Life

The banquet began with music and dancing. We stayed on as part of Pharaoh's court. The Pharaoh soon sent Hotep and Genie on missions to other towns in Egypt to clean them up, rid them of disease, but most of all to teach the towns' people how to stay in good health by preventing accidents and diseases.

Our first assignment was Deir "el-Basteta." I called it that because it was overrun with cats! It was the town for the workers of the Ramesseum that the Pharaoh was building. Because Ramses lived into his nineties, he had lots of time to build monuments to his own glory.

Monuments are fine; I think there's nothing wrong with them. However, the work that Hotep and Genie began—teaching people about how to preserve health and hygiene—impresses me much more.

Hotep and Genie were married and raised their children to respect both cats and snakes. In time, I learned to respect Khleo and, happily—though she teased me—she never bit me!

Meow!

PAWSCRIPT

Thousands of years ago, cats were worshipped as gods.
Cats have never forgotten this.
~ Anonymous

GLOSSARY

Adobe:
Adobe bricks are made out of clay or mud. Houses made out of these bricks are also called adobes.

Alabaster:
Alabaster is a naturally occurring white or transparent mineral. The ancient Egyptians carved alabaster into vases and jars.

Amulet:
An amulet is an ornament or piece of jewellery worn for good luck and as a charm against evil.

Ankh:
The Ankh is an ancient Egyptian hieroglyphic symbol of life or eternal life. It looks like a cross with a loop at the top, and many Egyptian gods are shown holding or wearing an ankh.

Annex:
An annex is something "added on," like an extension to a building. A country annexes another country when it takes over its lands and adds them to its own.

Cartouche:
In ancient Egyptian hieroglyphics, a cartouche was an oval symbol meaning "name." It often included a horizontal line on one end, which indicated the name inscribed inside the oval belonged to a Pharaoh or a member of royalty. Pharaohs

had two names—a birth name and a throne name—and both names were included in the cartouche.

Cataract:

A cataract is a shallow, stony section of a river that causes rapids. The "cataracts of the Nile" are six shallow sections, some of which can only be navigated during the flood season.

Demotic:

Demotic is a style of writing used by the ancient Egyptians starting around 650 BCE. It is more simplified than hieroglyphic symbols or hieratic writing. Demotic writing is one of the three scripts on the Rosetta Stone, the other two being Greek and Hieroglyphics.

Dung:

Dung is another word for the excrement or manure of animals.

Embalming:

Embalming is the practice of preserving human remains to delay decomposition. In ancient Egypt, special priests performed embalming and mummification.

Ennead:

Ennead means "a collection of nine things." In ancient Egypt, the Ennead of Heliopolis was a group of nine gods, who were the first gods. They were Atum; his children Shu and Tefnut; Shu and Tefnut's children Geb and Nut; and Geb and Nut's children Osiris, Isis, Seth, and Nephthys.

Eye of Horus:
The Eye of Horus is an ancient Egyptian symbol. It is a graphic of a falcon's eye; Horus, the Egyptian god of the sky, was often shown as a falcon.

Felucca:
Feluccas are wooden sail boats propelled by one or two sails, or oars, or both. Feluccas were the main mode of transportation in ancient Egypt, and are still used today on the Nile River, the Red Sea, and the Mediterranean Sea.

Fleabane:
Fleabane is a flowering plant belonging to the daisy family. In ancient Egypt, it was used to repel fleas.

Fumigate:
Fumigating means to treat or clean the air with fumes or smoke.

Granary:
A granary is a container or building used to store grain. In ancient Egypt, granaries were often made of clay.

Helmsman:
The helm of a ship is the steering system, which could be a wheel or a tiller. The helmsman is the person who steers the ship.

Heliopolis:
Heliopolis means "Eye of the Sun" and was the capital city of Egypt during the time of Pharaoh Ramses II. It is located in the Nile delta, where the city of Cairo is now.

Hieroglyph:

Hieroglyphs were symbols or pictures used as an early form of writing in ancient Egypt, especially on monuments and tombs. Hieroglyphics is one of three scripts found on the Rosetta Stone.

Hieratic:

Hieratic is an ancient Egyptian style of writing, mostly used by priests, that was easier to produce with ink on papyrus paper than hieroglyphics were.

House of Healing:

A House of Healing was an ancient Egyptian medical clinic where people went for diagnosis and treatment.

House of Life:

A House of Life was an ancient Egyptian place of learning. It was where scribes learned to write. It was also a medical school and library.

Ibis:

The sacred Ibis of Egypt was a bird, now extinct, that represented Thoth, the god of wisdom, knowledge, and writing.

Incense:

Incense is a material made from a gum or spice that produces a sweet or spicy smell when burned. The burning of incense was part of worshipping gods in temples.

Irrigation:
Irrigation is the system of supplying crops with water, often via channels or pipes. It was first invented in ancient Egypt during the time of King Menes of the First Dynasty.

Jackal:
The Egyptian jackal is a wolf-like breed of wild dog.

Javelin:
A javelin is a long, lightweight spear.

Mercenary:
A mercenary is a professional soldier hired to fight in a foreign army.

Mummy:
A mummy is a dried or embalmed dead body. Early Egyptians buried their dead in the hot desert sand, which dried or mummified the bodies. Later Egyptians embalmed their dead and wrapped them in linen strips.

Necropolis:
A necropolis is an ancient cemetery or place of burial.

Natron:
Natron is a natural mineral form of salt found in dried lake-beds. The ancient Egyptians used natron to dry out dead bodies in mummification procedures.

Obelisk:

Obelisks are a type of monument rising from a square base to a tapered top. In ancient Egypt, the obelisk symbolized Re (Ra), the sun god.

Papyrus:

Papyrus is a paper made from the inner stems of papyrus plants.

Pharaoh:

Pharaoh is the title given to an ancient Egyptian king or queen.

Pomegranate:

A pomegranate is a round, orange-sized fruit, with a tough red or yellow rind, and filled with seed sacs. In ancient Egypt, pomegranates were used for making wine, dying cloth in creams and yellows, and treating infections.

Proverbial:

A proverb is a short saying that expresses a truth or common experience, such as "the early bird catches the worm." The word "proverbial" means to use a proverb as an adjective to describe something.

Pungent:

The word "pungent" is used to describe something that has a very strong, often unpleasant, taste or smell.

Pylon:

A pylon is a gateway to an ancient Egyptian temple. It consists of two towers connected by a lower gate.

Pyramid:

Pyramids are a form of monument used as tombs in ancient Egypt. The pyramids in this story have a square base and four sides that taper up to a point.

Rosetta Stone:

The Rosetta Stone was discovered in Egypt in 1799 by a French soldier. It has an announcement engraved on it in three languages—Greek, hieroglyphics, and Demotic. By using the Demotic and Greek translations, the Rosetta Stone allowed Egyptologists to understand the meaning of the hieroglyphic characters.

Sabotage:

Sabotage is the deliberate damage or destruction of property.

Scarab:

The scarab beetle (sometimes called a dung beetle) was sacred to the ancient Egyptians. The word "scarab" refers to three things: the dung beetle; an image of the beetle on amulets or carvings; and a gem cut into the shape of the scarab beetle.

Scribe:

A scribe was a person who wrote important documents. In ancient Egypt, scribes were among the few people who could read and write.

Shaduf:

Developed during the Old Kingdom, a shaduf is a simple, hand-operated irrigation tool made from a tall pole, a bucket, and a counterweight. It is used to raise water from its source up to a field.

Sistrum:

A sistrum was a sacred, metal, jingling instrument used in ancient Egyptian religious ceremonies, especially those honouring Amon, Bastet, Hathor, and Isis. "Sistra" is the plural of sistrum.

Smallpox:

Smallpox is a contagious viral disease with fever and pus-filled blisters that can leave scars and cause blindness. Many mummies of Pharaohs have smallpox scars. Due to the success of smallpox vaccines, the disease was effectively eradicated in 1980.

Stela:

A stela is a slab of stone used as a marker or monument. Carved with inscriptions, they were often used as tombstones, temple monuments, or to announce victories and identify borders. "Stelae" is the plural of stela.

Sycamore:

Sycamores are a kind of fig tree that grows in the Middle East.

Theban Peak:

The Theban Peak is a naturally occurring, pyramid-shaped landmark in Egypt that overlooks the Valley of the Kings.

Tiller:
A tiller is a handle attached to the rudder of a boat, used for steering.

Triage:
Triage is the process of sorting injured people into categories for treatment, especially after a disaster or battle. The categories tell the doctors how seriously someone is injured and how urgently they require treatment.

Toilette:
Toilette is the activity of tending to one's appearance, and can include washing, dressing, and grooming.

Uraeus:
A Uraeus (you-ree-us) is the depiction of an Egyptian cobra or asp in an upright, rearing position. Representing royalty and supreme authority in ancient Egypt, the Uraeus was included on the headdresses of Pharaohs and gods.

Valley of the Kings:
The Valley of the Kings is located on the west bank of the Nile River across from Thebes. It is a sacred place where ancient Egyptians built tombs into the hillsides for their Pharaohs and their royal families.

Vermin:
Rodents and other small animals that are hard to get rid of—such as fleas, lice, bedbugs, and cockroaches—are known as vermin.

Vizier:

A vizier was a high-ranking official in ancient Egypt.

Whitewash:

Whitewash is a kind of white paint with antibacterial properties. It is made from lime (the mineral) and chalk mixed with water.

IMPORTANT DATES

Ancient Egypt is one of the oldest and longest-lasting civili-zations in human history, spanning more than 5,000 years. Historians often use one of two ways to describe the eras of this civilization. First, there are "the dynasties," which are years when a family of kings and queens ruled for generations. Second, there are "the kingdoms." There were three kingdoms—old, middle, and new—and an intermediate period between each. The timeline that follows includes both the dynasties and the kingdoms, and uses the dates published by Egyptologist Barbara Mertz, PhD, in *Red Land, Black Land*.

6000—5000 BCE: Neolithic Period
As northern Africa became more desert-like, early Egyptians moved and settled around the more fertile Nile River delta, bringing a more settled lifestyle to the region through agriculture.

5000—3110 BCE: Pre-Dynastic Period
Egyptians began to raise cattle and sheep, and to grow wheat and barley. Sails were added to boats, the main form of trans-portation. The first hieroglyphic wall paintings were created.

3110—2686 BCE: Early Dynastic Period
Dynasties I, II, and III
The Early Dynastic Period started with the rule of King Menes. He was the first to unite upper and lower Egypt, and his rule began the "era of dynasties." The first pyramid was built by Pharaoh Djoser and the famous architect Imhotep.

2686—2181 BCE: Old Kingdom
Dynasties IV, V, and VI

The three pyramids of Giza were built in honour of three kings. Khufu built the largest one, "the Great Pyramid"; his son Khafre built his own pyramid and added the Great Sphinx to guard it. Menkaure built the third pyramid. Rules of art were established that distorted perspective (according to modern eyes), but were pleasing to their cultural taste and lasted thousands of years. The fourth dynasty of Senusret was a time of peace, followed by weaker dynasties, poverty, and famine and the end of the Old Kingdom.

2181—2040 BCE: First Intermediate Period
Dynasties VII to X

Egypt was divided into upper and lower Egypt again.

2040—1786 BCE: Middle Kingdom
Dynasties XI and XII

The Middle Kingdom started with Pharaoh Mentuhotep reuniting upper and lower Egypt. Trading was expanded to include the Middle East and the island of Crete, and a large drainage and irrigation project created additional farmland.

1786—1570 BCE: Second Intermediate Period
Dynasties XIII to XVII

Many of the dynasties of this period were short in duration. The horse and chariot was brought to Egypt by the invading Hyksos from Asia. The Hyksos were forced out by the end of the second intermediate period.

1570—1085 BCE: New Kingdom
Dynasties XVIII to XX

The New Kingdom spanned the reigns of seventeen kings. The reunited Egyptian Empire reached its greatest prosperity, with the most land under its rule. Tuthmosis I was the first Pharaoh to be buried in the Valley of the Kings. Queen Hatshepsut built her temple in the Valley of the Kings. During his reign, Akhenaten changed Egyptian religion to a single god—Aten. His son Tutankhamen (the boy king) restored the multiple Egyptian gods. Ramses II became Pharaoh in his twenties, and ruled for sixty-seven years. He expanded Egypt's territory to Syria. This era ended with Ramses V.

1085—332 BCE: Late Period
Dynasties XXI to XXX

Late Period rulers included the high priests of Thebes, Libyan kings, and Nubian kings. The Persian conquest of 525 BCE brought an end to the rule of Egypt by Egyptians. Persians ruled Egypt for more than a hundred years.

332—30 BCE: Ptolemaic Period

Alexander the Great of Macedonia and the Greeks conquered Egypt. Ptolemy I, Alexander's general, became Pharaoh and the Ptolemaic Period began. The era ended with Queen Cleopatra VII.

30 BCE–364 CE: Roman Period

Roman rule continued until the Roman Empire collapsed.

IMPORTANT PEOPLE

Most of the historical references and characters in this story are true, based on the research of many Egyptologists. The fictional characters created for the story are Hotep, his mother Mayet, Hygenia, and Khleo, the asp.

Amen-hir-khopshef was the firstborn son of Ramses II and Queen Nefertari. As first born, he was the crown prince and heir, but did not become Pharaoh as he died before his father.

Hatshepsut (meaning "Foremost of Noble Ladies") was the fifth Pharaoh of the Eighteenth Dynasty and one of history's first recorded great women leaders. Her accomplishments include successfully re-establishing trade routes and commissioning many temples, buildings, and statues.

Imhotep was a multi-talented Egyptian who lived during the Third Dynasty (Dynasty III) under Pharaoh Djoser. He was one of the earliest architects, engineers, and physicians in history, and one of very few commoners who were given god-like status after death. He served as vizier to King Djoser, and created the Pyramid of Djoser, the first building made from cut stone; it is called the "step pyramid."

Khufu was the second Pharaoh of the Fourth Dynasty (Dynasty IV). He built the largest of the three pyramids at Giza, "The Great Pyramid." **Khafra** was the son of Khufu, and also a Pharaoh of the Fourth Dynasty. Khafra built the second largest pyramid at Giza, and the Great Sphinx.

Lufaa was the head priest at the Karnak Temple Complex during Pharaoh Ramses' Nineteenth Dynasty.

Merenptah was the fourth Pharaoh of the Nineteenth Dynasty (Dynasty XIX) and Ramses II's thirteenth son. He became Ramses' heir when his older brothers died before Ramses II.

Metu was a physician at Deir el-Medina, the ancient village where the builders and artisans lived while constructing the Valley of the Kings.

Nefertari was the first of the Great Royal Wives of Ramses II and an Egyptian queen. Her tomb is the largest and most decorated in the Valley of the Queens.

Paser held increasingly senior positions with Pharaohs Seti I and Ramses II, becoming a city governor, vizier, and a High Priest of Amun in Thebes. He oversaw the building of the tomb of Seti I in the Valley of the Kings.

Peseshet was one of the earliest recorded women physicians; she lived during the Fourth Dynasty. Egyptian records show she was referred to as "the lady director of lady physicians," which suggests there were other female doctors and midwives at that time.

Pre-hir-wonmef was the second son of Ramses II and Queen Nefertari.

Ramses II was the third Pharaoh of the Nineteenth Dynasty (Dynasty XIX) and ruled Egypt for 67 years. Known as "Ramses the Great," he is considered the most powerful Pharaoh of the Egyptian Empire. He built many buildings and temples in his honour, and had many wives, 111 sons, and 51 daughters.

Sennudjem was the construction foreman for the Valley of the Kings under Pharaohs Seti I and Ramses II.

Seti I was the second Pharaoh of the Nineteenth Dynasty (Dynasty XIX). He was the son of Ramses I and the father of Ramses II.

Tuya was an Egyptian queen, the Royal Wife of Pharaoh Seti I, and the mother of Ramses II.

IMHOTEP—THE TRUE FATHER OF MEDICINE?

Imhotep (im-hoe-tep), born in the 27th century BCE, was the "Leonardo da Vinci" of his time because, like Leonardo, he was multi-talented in many areas of the arts, science, technology, and medicine.

Imhotep was born a commoner near the ancient city of Memphis, but his family had the means to provide for his education, which began with writing. Imhotep wrote many books—some of a philosophical nature, including wise proverbs, but most of them about medicine.

He gained a reputation as a good physician and was called to Pharaoh Khasekhem's palace to attend the birth of his son. The queen had a long and difficult birth, but Imhotep saved her life and the life of the baby Djoser. While Imhotep saved the queen's life, his own wife tragically and ironically died the same day in childbirth. Imhotep buried her at Saqqara, and vowed he would one day build a monument over her grave. He kept his promise.

When Djoser became Pharaoh, he appointed Imhotep to be his vizier, a high-ranking official. At that time, physicians were well rounded in their education and the practice of medicine was tightly interwoven with religion. Thus, Imhotep was also a priest at the temple of Ptah in Memphis. Ptah was patron god of scribes. Two thousand years after his death, Imhotep was deified as the son of Ptah, and scribes would offer a drop of ink as tribute to Imhotep before beginning their work. Imhotep was also a student of engineering, math, and astronomy, as well as arts and crafts.

Soon after Imhotep became Djoser's vizier, the Pharaoh asked him to supervise the building of his monumental tomb. Imhotep then designed, invented the necessary tools, and built the step pyramid, the first large building to be made of stone. He built it in Saqqara where he had buried his wife.

During a seven-year famine, Pharaoh Djoser appealed to Imhotep for help. First, Imhotep advised the king to make sacrifices to Khnum, the god of water, to bring water to the fields. Then Imhotep developed a new irrigation system that supplied water, even when the Nile River was low. One reference said the shaduf (or water pole) was invented in the old kingdom era—perhaps by Imhotep. It scooped up water from the river into a jug, and using a counterweight lifted it to higher ground to ditches that carried the water to the fields. This apparatus is still used today in Africa and Asia. Imhotep didn't stop there. He brought about better food preservation and management of the fisheries. He brought an end to the famine. I wonder how much credit the Pharaoh was accorded for his sacrifices to Khnum!

Appointed as the high priest of the god Ptah of Memphis and of the sun god Re of Heliopolis, Imhotep improved the technique of mummification. He introduced the practice of removing the internal organs of the dead and placing them in stone or pottery jars for the person's use in the next life. He was well acquainted with anatomy, the circulation of blood, and the position and function of the organs. He treated more than two hundred diseases, including tuberculosis, gallstones, appendicitis, gout, and arthritis. He performed surgery and dentistry. He extracted medicines from plants.

Imhotep wrote many books on the practice of medicine. Only seven of the medical books have been found. There was a tragic fire in the Alexandria Library centuries ago, which could account for the tragic loss of the rest of his books.

Of Imhotep's medical books, one found by Edwin Smith tells of anatomical observations, ailments, and cures. Imhotep's medical writings were purely scientific and devoid of the magic and religion that was incorporated into the practice of medicine at the time.

The Edwin Smith papyrus addressed twenty-seven head, neck, and throat injuries; two collarbone injuries; three arm injuries; eight breastbone injuries; one tumour and abscess of the breast; one shoulder injury; and one spinal injury. The treatments included the use of suturing and splints.

The practice of medicine in ancient Egypt going back as far as 3000 BCE was so well developed that it astounded civilizations in Arabia, Greece, and Italy. Because he wrote his findings and practices down in papyrus scrolls, Imhotep is credited with much of the development of Egyptian medicine. He wasn't the only doctor of his time, but he is the most famous one and likely deserves the title of "Father of Medicine."

Hippocrates, who lived two thousand years later, is widely considered by many to be the Father of Medicine because he took the scientific approach one step further by eliminating the religious aspect and fostering the ethical practice of medicine as cited in the Hippocratic Oath.

The name Imhotep means, "he comes in peace."

AUTHOR'S NOTE TO PARENTS AND TEACHERS

Dear Parents and Teachers,

I have been asked why I have written so many stories about history as seen through the eyes of a cat. I have two reasons.

First, I am fulfilling the universal human wish to be a fly on the wall or an invisible witness. My cat is the proverbial fly on the wall because a cat has an amazing ability to stay incredibly still and blend into its surroundings. A cat can also hide in unexpected places.

Second, children need to have heroes to admire and to inspire them. I have chosen to depict heroes from real life, or inspired by real life, who are worthy of their attention. History is amazing. It relates to us the deeds and misdeeds of people. It then exposes the thinking that caused those good and bad actions by the visual means of arts and by written records.

No lesson from history is more amazing than the examples of man's creativity. For example, creative thinking brought about the pyramids and the harnessing of atomic energy.

In *Lexi Catt's Meowmoirs—Tales of Heroic Scientists*, I have focused on man's creative developments in the field of human health sciences. Though subjected to superstitions, religious taboos, political expediency, and financial greed, the development of mankind's understanding and preservation of human health is awe-inspiring. I salute the heroes who have courageously brought new insights to us, such as Imhotep, Hippocrates, Marie Curie, Leonardo da Vinci, Joseph Lister, and Linus Pauling.

Perhaps you too, and your children, will be amazed and inspired as we look at these heroes and their adventures through the eyes of a cat known as Lexi, Alexander Catt II.

Cheers,

Marian Keen

PS: From my research, I thought you might like to know some of the piquant tidbits, which I have included in the following pages; they are interesting but not necessary to the story.

THE MYTH OF THE BIRTH OF THE GODS

Primitive people had no scientific means to explain nature's events, so they made up explanations—creative, colourful, and magical explanations.

Where did the sun go when it disappeared below the western horizon? The Egyptians lived in the "upper" world that they could see, so the sun must go to the "under" world, which they couldn't see. So they invented "the underworld."

Where did people come from? Water was the source of life, so they believed that the world must have begun with water. The magic of creation was performed by a god who emerged from the water and spit out the first gods. That first god's name was Atum (very close to our word "atom"). Atum created the first male god, Shu, and the first female goddess, Tefnut. Shu and Tefnut then created Geb, the earth god, and Nut, the sky goddess. Geb and Nut created two sons and two daughters: Osiris, Seth, Nephthys, and Isis.

Thus, the first nine gods were created and were called the Ennead of Heliopolis ("Ennead" means a collection of nine things). From these nine gods came more than a hundred Egyptian gods.

Another source of stories or myths was oral history. People have always told stories about events and things that have happened. The repeating of stories became creative and, after a thousand years of retelling the same stories, the myths were born.

THE MYTH OF OSIRIS

According to myth, Osiris was the first ancient king of Egypt. He ruled wisely and kindly with his wife Isis by his side, and he taught the Egyptians the arts of civilization. But his brother Seth was jealous and determined to get rid of Osiris so he could rule Egypt himself.

So Seth secretly had a coffin custom-made to fit Osiris. It was beautifully decorated and much admired. Seth said he would give it to the person who fit in it. Many people tried, but they were either too big or too small. Osiris was persuaded to try, and when he lay in it, it fit him perfectly. Seth closed the lid, nailed it shut, and threw the coffin into the river, drowning his brother. Seth then became ruler—a nasty ruler.

Isis searched for Osiris and finding his body used her magic powers to restore Osiris to life.

Seth found Osiris again, and killed him a second time. He cut Osiris's body into pieces and scattered them all over Egypt.

With the help of her sister Nephthys, Isis found the pieces, and put Osiris back together, although she could not bring him back to life a second time. She wrapped his body in linen for burial and his trip to the underworld. This was the first mummy. Osiris became ruler of the underworld. To avenge his father Osiris, Horus fought Seth and won, and so became the new ruler of Egypt. Horus was a kind and wise ruler.

Osiris was god of upper Egypt, and wore a white crown. Seth was god of the north, and wore a red crown. The conflict between them mirrored the conflict between the two kingdoms of upper and lower Egypt. After Horus unified Egypt, the kings wore the double crown of red and white.

THE EGYPTIAN GODS

The Ancient Egyptian religion honoured more than a hundred gods and goddesses, who ruled over many aspects of nature and daily living. The Egyptians sought the protection of their gods and constructed temples in their honour. They were very polytheistic (*poly* means "many" and *theo* means "god").

Sophisticated theorizing and myths from dozens of temples over thousands of years produced many explanations for every natural phenomenon. The Egyptians considered all interpretations valid and were very open minded to others' ways of thinking.

Look at this example of Egyptian thinking and logic:

- The sun was reborn every morning, and represented everlasting life.
- Any orb or ball shape was related to the sun.
- The dung beetle was observed pushing a ball of dung ahead of him.
- The Egyptians believed the dung beetle's offspring was in the ball of dung, and that the beetle's young would be born like the sun was every morning.
- Therefore, the dung beetle became a sun god, called Khephri.

Adding to the confusion of these stories and myths is the fact that many gods shared characteristics, duties, and animal representations with other gods.

Some of the main Egyptian gods and their attributes follow.

Ammut was a ferocious beast, known as the "Devourer of Shades," and was depicted as a combination of three man-eating animals, with a crocodile's head, a lion's torso, and the hindquarters of a hippopotamus. Ammut lived near the scales of justice in the underworld, and she ate the hearts of the dead who, because they were found to be unworthy, did not pass Osiris's judgement.

Amun was the god of wind, and one of the more powerful Egyptian gods. He was depicted as a human wearing a twin, plumed headdress with a solar disk. Later, Amun was merged with the sun god, Re, thus becoming even more powerful as Amun-Re. Amun was associated with a species of ram sheep that had downward-curling horns. Rows of these ram statues lead up to the Karnak Temple, which became a centre of learning.

Anubis was the jackal-headed god of the dead, funerals, and embalming (preserving human remains). Wild dogs called jackals were often seen in cemeteries, so the animals were associated with the dead. Embalmers even wore jackal masks during their rites. Anubis appears as a human with a black, wild-dog head. He was a key figure in the judging of the dead, and supervised the "weighing of the heart" ceremony (see *Maat*).

Atum arose from the creation flood as the first god, and then spat out nine other gods. Thus, the legend of creation began, and these original gods were called the Ennead. Atum later merged with Re, god of the Sun, and became Atum-Re, and so became the supreme solar-creator. Atum appears as a human wearing the double-crown of Egypt. This crown shows sovereignty over all of Egypt and, therefore, the whole world.

Bastet was the goddess of cats, a protector of mothers, and a ferocious war goddess. She was shown as a woman with a cat's or lioness's head. A temple to Bastet was built during the reigns of Khufu and Khafre, and Khafre built the Great Sphinx to guard his pyramid. Though cats were hunters and killed snakes, they were also tamed and considered sacred.

Bes was a fierce-looking, bandy-legged dwarf god, with a lion's mane and protruding tongue. He was a protector of mothers, children, homes, music, and dancing. Bes often accompanied the goddess of childbirth, **Taweret**, who was shown as a pregnant hippopotamus; and also protected mothers and children. Both were popular household gods who brought good luck.

 **Geb** was the god of the earth, and the Egyptians believed that earthquakes were caused by Geb's laughter. He was one of the original nine gods of the Ennead. He married Nut, the sky goddess, and they had four children: Osiris, Isis, Nephthys, and Seth.

 **Hathor** was the most important of the goddesses associated with motherhood, and was identified with beauty, music, and love. She is depicted as a woman with cow's horns holding the sun. The Egyptians believed she protected the sun during the hours of darkness, so she was called "Lady of the West." Her image was used on the handles of mirrors and on rattle-like musical instruments called *sistra*.

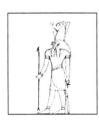 **Horus** was one of the earliest gods in ancient Egypt. The son of Osiris and Isis, he was associated with kingship, and was the god of the sky, war, and hunting. He is depicted as a man with a falcon's head, and represented majesty and power. The Eye of Horus (eye of a falcon) was a symbol of protection and power, which was also used in early math. Various parts of the Eye of Horus depict fractions from one half to one sixty-fourth. These fractions were used to record the amounts of ingredients used in preparing medicines.

When Horus was a child, he was called **Harpokrates** and shown as a child with his finger in his mouth. The Greeks later adopted this god as their god of silence. Perhaps the name Harpokrates was adopted by the ancestors of the Greek physician, Hippocrates.

Isis was the sister and wife of Osiris; mother of Horus; and goddess of magic, marriage, and healing. Her healing powers are depicted in the way she brought Osiris back to life when his brother Seth had killed him. She changed into a bird when she looked for Osiris and is often shown with wings. She is also shown in sculptures with Horus as a baby on her lap (Harpokrates).

Khephri was a sun god in the form of a scarab beetle, and god of rebirth, sunrise, and beetles. He was depicted as a man with a beetle head, or simply as a beetle, and appeared on decorated furniture, and in paintings, jewellery, and amulets.

Khnum was one of the earliest gods; a potter god of creation; and god of the source and floods of the Nile River. He is depicted as a man with a ram's head, often seated at a potter's wheel. Khnum moulded all living things on his potter's wheel using clay from the Nile, and allotted each a lifespan or "fate." When he tired of this, he put a potter's wheel in every female to continue the work of creation.

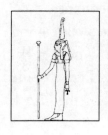

Maat was the goddess of truth and justice, and participated in the "weighing of the heart" ceremony when someone died. Wearing a head-dress of ostrich feathers, Maat's "feather of truth" was placed on one side of the scales at judgement time, and the dead person's heart on the other. If the heart was lighter than the feather (i.e., free of bad deeds), the person could enter the underworld and eternal life. But if bad deeds had made the heart heavy, the person was denied everlasting life, and the demon goddess Ammut ate the heart.

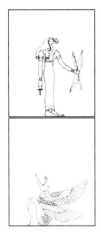

Nekhbet was the vulture goddess and protector of upper Egypt. Her counterpart was **Wadjet**, the cobra goddess and protector of lower Egypt. Together, they were called "the two ladies." Their animal forms were displayed on the respective Pharaohs' headdresses, and when upper and lower Egypt were united under one Pharaoh, both the vulture and cobra were included.

Nephthys was a goddess of the original Ennead "nine," and the sister and wife of Seth. When Seth killed their brother Osiris, Nephthys helped Isis collect Osiris's body parts, and she became a protector of the dead.

Nut (pronounced noot) was the sky goddess, and protector of the dead. She swallowed the sun each evening and gave birth to it every dawn. When she ascended to the sky, she wore a blue dress, giving the sky its colour. Nut was the sister and wife of the earth god, Geb. According to myth, Nut was cursed—not to have children all 360 days of the year. But she won five extra days in a game of dice with Thoth, the god of time, and had five children: Osiris, Isis, Seth, Nephthys, and Horus the Elder.

Osiris was the god of the dead and the afterlife. He was the father of Horus. Twice he was murdered by his brother Seth, who was jealous of Osiris for being the Pharaoh. When his wife and sister Isis couldn't revive him the second time, Osiris became king of the underworld. He wore the white crown of Upper Egypt.

Ptah was the creator god of Memphis, the first capital city of a unified Egypt. It was believed that Ptah created the world by his thoughts and utterances. As a creator and intellectual, he invented the arts and was the god of crafts and craftsmen. Egyptians believed he was the father of the famous architect and physician Imhotep.

Re (or **Ra**) was the god of creation and the Sun, and the most important god in ancient Egypt. He had the body of a man and the head of a hawk or falcon, and travelled across the sky by day and through the underworld at night. Pharaohs used "Son of Re" in their titles. The pyramids enabled Re to take Pharaohs to the sky after death. Many of the temples built to honour Re featured an obelisk as a symbol of the Sun god.

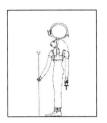

Sekhmet, meaning "powerful one," was the daughter of Re; protector of Pharaohs; and goddess of fire, war, and healing. She had a woman's body with the head of a lioness, the fiercest animal to the Egyptians. Considered one of Re's eyes, Sekhmet carried out his vengeance. She drove sickness from the body so was associated with healing, and was the wife of Ptah.

Seth (or **Set**) was one of the original nine deities, and god of violence, storms, chaos, and evil. These negatives were believed to be necessary for a balanced world. Seth was shown as a dog-like animal with a long snout and a forked tail. On his good side, he travelled with Re to protect the sun god from the serpent Apophis. Seth was jealous of his brother Osiris, and killed him twice. Osiris's son Horus sought revenge against Seth, and they fought for eighty years.

Shu was one of the original nine deities, and god of light, air, wind, fog, and clouds. He is depicted as a man with feathers on his head. As the god of light, he was responsible for the separation of night and day, and of the worlds of the living and the dead. He was the brother and husband of Tefnut, goddess of moisture, and the father of their two children, sky goddess Nut and earth god Geb.

Sobek was a protector of Pharaohs, and god of the Nile River, crocodiles, fertility, and the military. He is depicted as a man with a crocodile head, and was thought to be as powerful as the god Horus. His temple was located at the first cataract in the Nile River.

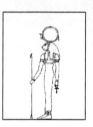

Tefnut was the goddess of moisture, dew, and rain, and was one of the original Ennead. She was usually shown as a lioness, or as a woman with a lion's head. She was the sister and wife of Shu, the god of air. Their two children were Nut, the sky goddess, and Geb, the earth god.

Thoth was originally a moon god, and because the moon's phases impacted rituals and daily life, he became associated with time and the calendar. He was also a god of wisdom, knowledge, and magic. Thoth was often seen holding a reed pen, and was the official recorder of the weighing of the heart ceremony. It was believed he invented hieroglyphic writing and wrote forty-two books of wisdom. He was depicted as a man with either the head of a baboon or an ibis.

JUDGEMENT OF THE DEAD

The ancient Egyptians believed in life after death, so they preserved or embalmed the bodies of their dead for the afterlife. Internal organs were removed and placed in Canopic jars, made of limestone or pottery, and sealed. Each body was next dried for days, submerged in natron, a naturally occurring salt from river beds. After that, the body was wrapped in linen strips and placed in a wooden coffin. This was put into a sarcophagus (a stone coffin-like container) decorated with inscriptions and designs. The sarcophagus was then placed into an underground chamber called a tomb. The tombs were supplied with all the necessities for life after death, including instructions for the deceased to navigate the underground passage to his eternal life. In the valleys west of Thebes, tombs were dug out of the steep hills for the burial of kings and queens.

However, it was believed that the dead were subject to the "Last Judgement." The judge was Osiris who ruled the underworld with his wife Isis by his side. There was a jury of forty-two gods. The deceased was escorted to the judgement scene by the jackal god Anubis. Thoth, the scribe god, recorded the verdict. In the centre was a big set of scales with Maat the goddess of truth and justice standing nearby. Her feather occupied one side of the scales as a measurement. The defendant's heart was placed on the other side of the scales. The heart was witness to all the deeds of the deceased and so was measured against truth, represented by a feather. The deceased pleaded his case denying the many wrongdoings. It was in his favour to speak the truth and repent of misdeeds.

Ammut, the Devourer of Shades crouching near the scales was a beast with a head of a crocodile, the midsection of a lion, and the hind end of a hippopotamus.

Osiris reached his verdict by the "witness of the heart." Because the heart was the witness to all the deeds of the deceased, it was the measure of the dead's morality. Simply put, if the heart was heavy, the person had been bad. If the heart was light, the deceased had led a moral life.

If the heart was lighter than Maat's feather, the defendant continued on his journey to everlasting life. If the heart was heavier, the defendant could plead on his mother's heart, but if that failed, the beast god Ammut ate his heart and the defendant was denied the afterlife and died a second time. This was dreaded and feared by all Egyptians.

The Egyptians did not fear dying the first time because they so thoroughly prepared for it, confident in the fact that they would gain everlasting life. The preparations for the afterlife placed with the deceased are the reason why the tombs of the Egyptians are so full of information about these ancient people.

THE ROSETTA STONE
UNLOCKING THE ANCIENT LANGUAGE OF EGYPT

At first, dating back to around 3300 BCE, language was written in Egypt through pictures. Called hieroglyphs, these pictures were carved into clay and stone.

In neighbouring Sumeria, writers used a wedge-shaped stick called a stylus to press symbols into wet clay. Varying the directions and multiple marks, writers could write clearly and quickly. This was termed "cuneiform writing." The Egyptians adopted this idea with their own hieroglyphic signs.

But hieroglyphs were cumbersome and time-consuming to create, so Egyptian priests took shortcuts when writing with ink on papyrus, a paper made from the inner stems of papyrus plants. These simpler signs were called "hieratic writing."

Around 650 BCE, men in business and government took further shortcuts for efficiency. Their business style of writing was called "Demotic writing" and became more commonly used.

When it was discovered that symbols could represent sounds, letters were born. At first, only consonants were used. This is reflected in many Egyptian words such as "swn" for doctor. There were about twenty-two consonants. The use of these consonant letters spread around the Mediterranean although each country gave credit for their invention to their gods. The Egyptians credited their god Thoth. Finally, the Greeks invented vowels to complete the first "true alphabet" that had both vowels and consonants.

The ancient Egyptian language evolved several times over

the millennia, from hieroglyphs, to hieratic and Demotic writing, to Coptic language (used by Egyptian Christians) which phased out of daily use in the 17th century when Arabic became more commonly used.

During the French Revolutionary Wars, Napoleon invaded Egypt for strategic purposes. In addition to taking his army, Napoleon took 175 professors to collect and study ancient relics. In 1799, a Napoleonic soldier discovered the Rosetta Stone, inscribed with three kinds of writing—hieroglyphics, Greek, and one unknown, later identified as Demotic.

Soon after, French scholar and gifted linguist Jean-Francois Champollion became fascinated with ancient Egypt. He hoped one day to read the hieroglyphs, which he thought mysterious.

Many world scholars studied the Rosetta Stone, including Jean-Francois. He could read many languages including Latin, Greek, Hebrew, Arabic, Persian, and Coptic. He deduced that the stone's message was a public notice, meant for all to read. Jean-Francois pieced together the proper names and common words using the Greek portion of the stone, and was able to develop a translation of the hieroglyphics—he published his decipherment of the Rosetta Stone in 1822. His keys to the stone's hieroglyphs led others to translate the writings in the tombs and on monuments, *stelae*, and temples.

The Pharaohs' Crowns

Pharaohs in ancient Egypt wore a variety of crowns or head-dresses. Several included the image over the forehead of a rearing cobra snake; the image is called a Uraeus.

None of these crowns has survived.

The White Crown (or Hedjet) was tall, white, and rounded at the top. It represented the Pharaohs' rule over upper Egypt, in the south.

The Red Crown (or Deshret) was red and basket-shaped, and represented the Pharaohs' rule over lower Egypt, in the north. The Red Crown included a Uraeus.

The Double Crown (or Pschent) was the name given to the wearing of both the White Crown and the Red Crown together. The Double Crown represented the Pharaohs' rule over a united Egypt, and included a Uraeus.

The Blue Crown (or Khepresh) was made of cloth or leather, and decorated with bronze or gold, and a Uraeus. It was worn during battle and at ceremonial events.

The Nemes Headdress was a blue and gold striped, heavy cloth, tied at the back of the head like a scarf. Two flaps hung down both sides of the head, and it included a Uraeus. The Nemes headdress was worn for less formal occasions.

The Vulture Crown: Queens favoured wearing the vulture crown, which looked as though a bird had wrapped its wings around the queen giving her a hug on her head. Sometimes a moon disk or ostrich feathers were added.

Queen Nefertiti's Blue Crown: Queen Nefertiti was the wife of Pharaoh Akhenaten (the father of King Tut), and she was the only one to wear her blue crown. The sculpture of her wearing this crown is so famous, and so beautiful, that it bears mention here.

ANCIENT EGYPTIAN COSMETICS

Beauty was important to the ancient Egyptians. Many aspects of their lives were governed by magic and gods, and cosmetics were no exception. Part of daily living, cosmetics were included in the tombs to provide the dead with everything they needed for a beautiful afterlife.

Both men and women used toilette articles such as metal mirrors, razors, combs, and pots and jars that contained cosmetics, creams, and ointments. These were kept in low chests.

The two most common kinds of make-up were the grey galena or black kohl used to outline the eyes to create an almond-shape and the green eyeshadow made from the mineral malachite. These enhanced the eyes and were believed to ward off eye diseases and infections. These colours were applied with a bone, a wooden rod, or a finger.

Red ochre, a mineral found in clay from the Nile, was mixed with water and used on the lips and cheeks; and henna was used to colour fingernails.

Egypt was well known for its perfumes. Many fragrant ingredients such as the leaves, blossoms, and roots of plants like irises, roses, and cinnamon were added to a base of plant oils. Perfumes could have ten or more ingredients and were kept as liquids or mixed with waxes or fats to make creams and lotions. Scented ointments were applied to the skin to keep it moist in the dry climate. On special occasions, perfumed wax cones were placed on top of wigs to melt down over the body, giving off a delicate scent.

Women wore their hair in various styles from mid-length to long. They often wore braided wigs. Men wore their hair short and also wore wigs. Boys had shaved heads with a single braided side-lock until they became adults.

ANCIENT EGYPTIAN CLOTHING

Egyptian summers were hot and winters were mild, so clothing was minimal and made of light cloth to keep the body cool. Linen was made from the flax plant, and its quality could be varied from coarse canvas to delicate gauze. The flax plant fibres were spun into linen thread, and then the cloth was woven on looms. Wool was considered unclean, and cotton and silk were rare.

Women wore form-fitting dresses with wide straps over the shoulders. Mantles (loose overgarments) and sashes were added.

Sheer, delicately pleated robes were also worn, with cape-like covers that were cross tied, giving the effect of elbow-length sleeves. Bright embroidered sashes held these open garments in place.

Men wore short skirts or kilts, often pleated, sometimes with collarless shirts.

Shoes were seldom worn; people went barefoot. Simple leather sandals were worn on special occasions.

Ancient Egyptian Medicine

In today's world, many women have taken doses of medicine to balance their hormones, and these medicines have their origins in horse urine.

For years, people have turned to antibiotics prescribed by their physicians to fight bacterial infections; some of these antibiotics have come from bread mould.

Vaccines are sourced from the diseases themselves.

Other medicines are made from equally surprising plant and animal ingredients. And while they can help fight infection and disease, they can also be extremely dangerous if taken in incorrect doses.

That is why one should never, ever take someone else's medication, and also why one must follow doctors' orders according to how much and when to take the medicine. Listen to your doctor and do exactly as you are instructed.

Before you read the following, keep in mind the sources of our modern medicines.

Since the beginning of humankind, people have endeavoured to preserve their health and restore their bodies from injury and disease. This is the practice and art of medicine. Understanding the source of disease and result of inherent disorders is the basis of the science of medicine. Overwhelming strides have been made in the last century due to the development of technology, whereas in primitive times explanations were magical in nature.

Ancient people explained the inexplicable with myths, gods, and magic. Early physicians used these beliefs as part of their treatment of the whole person. That is, they let patients believe it was magic or the result of offerings and prayers to their god of choice. This was the art of medicine.

Even today, doctors do not explain the biochemistry of a medication to their patients. But there is still the element of trust in the art of medical practice.

The sands of Egypt caused dental problems because it covered vegetables and was used as a cutting agent in the milling of bread. Teeth became worn, ground down from chewing gritty foods. This also affected the gums, causing periodontal disease. According to an ancient Egyptian papyrus book, the remedy for this was a mixture of cumin, frankincense, and carob-pod pulp, ground to a powder and applied to the tooth.

Teeth were worn down so much that the dental pulp became exposed and infected. An abscess followed, or sometimes became a cyst in the jaw. Because the surfaces of the teeth were worn, the joints of the jaw became abnormal as well. So much dental infection caused bad breath. To sweeten the breath, they mixed frankincense, myrrh, and cinnamon bark, boiled them with honey, and shaped them into pellets. This was also used as a house fumigator.

Personal cleanliness was essential to the Egyptians. All washed frequently, especially before every meal. Having no soap and little water, they used a refreshing body scrub made from powdered calcite, red natron, salt, and honey. Ointments kept the skin soft. Deodorants were made from ground carob-pod pulp, or from a mix of porridge and incense rolled into pellets and rubbed onto the skin.

In the early dynastic period, there were forty-two sacred books that summarized the medical field. They covered medicine, anatomy, diseases, surgery, and remedies.

During the Old Kingdom that followed, the medical profession became organized into ranks and specialties. An ordinary doctor was lowest in rank. Above him was the overseer of doctors; then the chief of doctors; he was followed by the eldest of doctors and finally the inspector of doctors. Physicians were separate from surgeons. Surgeons were known as "priests of the goddess Sekhmet."

During Pharaoh Djoser's reign, Imhotep was his chief physician. The only lady doctor known was Peseshet (fourth dynasty) but her title, "lady director of lady physicians," indicates there were others. The House of Life was the medical study centre located in some temples. The sources of many medications were grown in an herb garden beside the temple.

Religion played a major role in the treatment of a patient. Physicians appealed to the particular god needed for the patient. They poured water over a god's statue and gave the water to the patient to drink to help the cure. Amulets were worn to keep away disease and statuettes of gods were kept in homes. All these measures lent comfort and created a positive attitude in the patient.

There are many references to surgical stitching and adhesive tape made from linen. Linen was used to make bandages and sutures. Needles were made of copper, and sometimes reeds. Surgical tools included medical shears, knives, saws, hooks, forceps, and scalpels. Doctors were aware of the difference between clean wounds and infected wounds. They used a mixture of ibis fat, fir oil, and crushed peas as an ointment to clean an infected wound.

When a broken bone needed casting, a cast was made from cow's milk mixed with barley or acacia leaves, gum, and water. Bark splints and bandages were also used.

Knives and scalpels used in surgery were made of bronze or copper and were heated to prevent the patient from bleeding. According to an ancient papyrus, "if it bleeds a lot, you must burn it with fire." Reeds were also used for cutting, were disposable, and readily available.

Egyptian physicians were greatly respected even outside Egypt. They were often sent by the Pharaoh to foreign countries, upon request, as a gesture of goodwill.

Medical texts written on papyrus from ancient Egypt were found by Edwin Smith of America in 1862 and by George Ebers of Germany in 1873.

The Edwin Smith Papyrus describes forty-eight trauma wounds to the head (possibly war injuries) and depicts the triage sorting for dealing with disasters, much like today's approach. The Egyptians counted a patient's pulse and compared it to their own. They recognized its connection to the heart.

The George Ebers Papyrus mentions five hundred substances used in medical treatment: "fifty-five of the prescriptions feature urine and feces as the main component."

Narcotics from the poisonous mandrake plant were used to put a patient to sleep. Many materials were imported from outside Egypt. For example, the resin from fir trees was used as an antiseptic. Oil of fir was used to clean infected wounds. Aloe was used to clear stuffy noses. Cinnamon was used to heal bleeding gums and mixed in incense with myrrh and frankincense.

Incense was used to fumigate and sweeten the air. The burning of incense produces phenol or carbolic acid, later used by Joseph Lister to provide an antiseptic operating room. The formula from the Ebers papyrus to sweeten the smell of houses or clothes was to "grind and mix together dry myrrh, pignon, frankincense, rush-nut, bark of cinnamon, Phoenician reed, and liquid styrax. A little of this mixture was then placed over a fire."

Fleabane, an antibacterial substance, was used to fumigate a space and to drive fleas from the house.

The term "powder of green pigment" referred to various green minerals and salts: to the green stone malachite, to copper carbonate, to copper silicate, and to a powder made from mixing sand, natron salt, and copper minerals. The latter was cheaper and was used as eye paint and to prevent eye infections. It was also used in ointments to clean wounds, because copper prevents the penetration of bacteria into wounds.

The black pigment also used as eye make-up and a salve was made from a lead sulphide called galena. In spite of using this, the lead intake of Egyptian bodies was a hundred times less than modern people absorb.

The drug called "spn" was often used to calm crying babies. It was primarily made from a plant which is used today to manufacture prescription painkillers. From the Ebers papyrus, this plant was mixed with "fly dung from the wall, made into a paste, strained and drunk for four days. The crying will cease instantly." It seems these ingredients must have been dissolved in water.

Five hundred recorded prescriptions and remedies included honey. Honey is highly resistant to bacterial growth because it dries bacterial cells. Honey is an antibiotic and it promotes faster healing than conventional treatments of wounds, burns, and ulcers.

The Egyptians thought that feces contained a horrific substance they called "whdw" or "the rots." But they believed in treating "like with like," which is the basis of modern homeopathic medicine. So mud and excrement were used in many medications. The Egyptians thought whdw infected sores, ulcers, and wounds all over the body, so that's why whdw itself was used in treatments. Sometimes it worked.

In the late 19th century, Louis Pasteur discovered that microorganisms produce substances with antimicrobial action. So bacteria living in humans and animals release their excrement into the feces and urine, which become a source of antibiotics. In fact, some antibiotics have been found in soil, which may explain why mud was used by the Egyptians in their medical treatments.

Doctors of ancient Egypt prepared their own medicines. A medicine or remedy was put into a container with the prescription written on it. In modern times, pharmacies and drug companies do this for the physician.

The Egyptians developed the concept of the prescription. As they discovered which drugs were useful and which were harmful or deadly, they figured out what proportions worked best. They weighed and measured according to the pictorial representation of the Eye of Horus. Each component of the formal drawing of the Eye of Horus represents the dosage proportion of the prescription.

In today's pharmacies, the character "Rx" designates the word "prescription" and it comes directly from the Eye of Horus.

THE BATTLE OF KADESH
AND THE FIRST RECORDED PEACE AGREEMENT

For more than 3,000 years, the Egyptians lived in peace. Their land was protected on the east and west by formidable deserts, and to the north by the Mediterranean Sea. They ruled Nubia to the south. This effectively kept out intruders, and the people had everything they needed. They were content.

Peace ended when the Hyksos, a warrior tribe from Asia, conquered Egypt. It was 150 years later, at the beginning of the New Kingdom (1570 BCE), that the Hyksos were driven out, and Egyptian leaders became more aggressive in maintaining and expanding their borders.

The expansion of their borders extended to the City of Kadesh (in modern Syria) several times over the following hundreds of years.

In 1274 BCE, Ramses II travelled to the City of Kadesh to once again reclaim the former Egyptian border from the northern Hittites.

Both Ramses II and the Hittite King had raised large armies.

The Egyptian army was mostly infantry (foot soldiers), fighting with javelins and short swords. They wore helmets and armoured tunics, and carried ox-hide shields on wooden frames. The army also used small, lightweight chariots that carried two men—a warrior with a bow and arrows, and a driver.

The Hittites had far more chariots, and their chariots were larger, heavier, and able to carry three men—a driver, a warrior, and a shield bearer. Warriors carried curved swords and spears. The chariots were used to break up their enemy's infantry lines before their own infantry charged.

Ramses planned his route along the Mediterranean coast, east and then north to Syria, following the Orontes River.

Ramses' army of 35,000 men had six divisions:

- one division was Ramses' personal bodyguard;
- four divisions were called Amon, Re, Ptah, and Set, after Egyptian gods; and
- one division was a reserve force of well-trained mercenaries, called Na'arum.

The Hittites army of 27,500 men was composed of:

- 10,500 men in 3,500 chariots
- 17,000 men in infantry

Ramses sent the Na'arum toward the Mediterranean as he continued east then north. As the Egyptian forces prepared to cross the river, two men approached claiming loyalty to Egypt. They told Ramses that the Hittite leader had retreated to the north. Ramses hurried to take control of the City of Kadesh while it was unguarded. He crossed the Orontes River, passed through a forest, and reached clear ground near the city. As he waited for his Amon division to arrive, he built a fortified camp.

Meanwhile, two Hittite scouts were captured and beaten for information. The two confessed that Ramses was in a trap. The Hittite army was huge, and hidden, waiting to attack, and Ramses had worsened his position by advancing too quickly while his other divisions lagged behind.

Ramses was not worried. His Amon division had arrived. His Re division was just south, coming out of the forest, so he had half his army. He sent a messenger to hurry the Set and Ptah divisions.

The Re division emerged from the forest, and—not expecting an immediate battle—the infantry's shields were slung over their backs. Immediately, 2,500 of the Hittite chariots attacked them, taking them by surprise, and wiping out most of the Re division. A few of the Re hid in the forest, and some, including his two sons, raced their chariots to reach Ramses and advise him of the surprise attack. Ramses immediately ordered one son to take the royal wives and children from the camp and hide them. He had barely enough time to organize the rest of his men before the Hittites surrounded them and attacked, crashing the barrier of Egyptian shields. Ramses' royal bodyguard division jumped at the enemy horses, dragging many Hittite chariots to a stop, effectively blocking more enemy chariots.

Though Ramses' own chariot was ready to go with its horses in harness, his driver had fled in terror. So Ramses wrapped the reins around his body and shouted to his horses, Victory and Mut. Ramses called to Amun for strength and charged the Hittites. He circled around them, returning to his camp where the Hittites were busy looting, thinking they had already won. Ramses and his other son rallied his personal bodyguard division, including chariots, and led a charge against the Hittite force, driving them back across the river.

While Ramses was attacking the Hittite chariots, the Na'arum division arrived and attacked the Hittite infantry who continued looting the camp. The Na'arum were well-trained, armed with swords and spears, and they overwhelmed the Hittites.

The Hittite leader dispatched a thousand more chariots against Ramses, expecting an easy victory. However, the heavier Hittite chariots had first to cross the river and climb the river bank, slowing their battle speed and preventing them from forming themselves into a fighting unit. Ramses' men picked them off a few at a time. The battle continued for three hours, and in Ramses' own words, "there were none who escaped me."

At this point, the Ptah division emerged from the forest and the Hittites retreated. Ramses gathered his army and headed for Damascus. Both sides claimed victory, but Ramses was accorded the status of hero. He erected stelae to proclaim his victory.

At various times over the next fifteen years, both the Egyptians and the Hittites attempted to claim the walled City of Kadesh. But being so evenly matched, neither side could solidly defeat the other.

In 1280 BCE, a new Hittite leader invited the Egyptians to the first summit conference between two equally matched powers. Ramses II and the Hittite leader signed history's first recorded international peace agreement. Today, the original Kadesh Peace Agreement is displayed at the Istanbul Archeology Museum in Turkey, and a replica hangs on the wall of the United Nations in New York City.

The past is never dead,
not even is it past.
~ Pharaoh Ramses II

BIBLIOGRAPHY

BOOKS AND MAGAZINE ARTICLES

Brown, Chip. "The Search for Cleopatra." *National Geographic*, July 2011.

Claiborne, Robert. *The Birth of Writing*. New York: Time-Life Books Inc., 1974.

Crosher, Judith. *Ancient Egypt*. London: Hamlyn Children's Books, 1992.

Davidovits, Joseph and Margie Morris. *The Pyramids: An Enigma Solved*. New York: Dorset Press, 1990.

Dee, Jonathan. *Chronicles of Ancient Egypt*. London: Collins and Brown Ltd., 1998.

Desroches-Noblecourt, Christiane. *The Great Pharaoh Ramses II and His Time: An Exhibition of Antiquities from the Egyptian Museum, Cairo at the Great Hall of Ramses II, Expo 86 Vancouver, BC, Canada May 12—October 13, 1986*. Montreal: Canada Exim Group, 1986.

Estabrook, Barry. "Poured Pyramids: A New Explanation for an Ancient Mystery." *Equinox Magazine*.

Folsom, Franklin. *The Language Book* New York: Grosset & Dunlap, 1963.

Gore, Rick. "Pharaohs of the Sun." *National Geographic*, April 2001.

Hamilton, R. *Ancient Egypt: Kingdom of the Pharaohs*. Bath: Parragon Publishing, 2005.

Harris, Nathaniel. *Everyday Life in Ancient Egypt*. New York: Franklin Watts, 1994.

Hawass, Zahi. "Egypt's Forgotten Treasures." *National Geographic*, January 2003.

Hawass, Zahi. "Tut's Family Secrets." *National Geographic*, September 2010.

Klum, Mattias. "King Cobras." *National Geographic*, November 2001.

Lemonick, Michael. "Secrets of the Lost Tomb." *Time Magazine*, May 1995.

Macdonald, Fiona. *Women in Ancient Egypt: The Other Half of History*. New York: Peter Bedrick Books, 1999.

McNeill, Sarah. *Ancient Egyptian People*. Brookfield: Millbrook Press, 1997.

Mertz, Barbara. *Red Land, Black Land*. New York: Peter Bedrick Books, 1990.

Metropolitan Museum of Art. *Treasures of Tutankhamun*. New York: Metropolitan Museum of Art, 1976.

Millard, Anne. *Pyramids: Egyptian, Nubian, Mayan, Aztec, Modern*. New York: Larousse Kingfisher Chambers Inc., 1996.

Morell, Virginia. "The Pyramid Builders." *National Geographic*, November 2001.

Musso, Carlos. "Imhotep: The Dean Among the Ancient Egyptian Physicians—An Example of a Complete Physician." *Humane Medicine*, 2005.

Reeves, Carole. *Egyptian Medicine*. Buckinghamshire: Shire Publications Ltd., 2001.

Romer, John. *Romer's Egypt: A New Light on the Civilization of Ancient Egypt*. London: The Rainbird Publishing Group Ltd., 1982.

Short, Bruce. "Imhotep and the Origins of Ancient Egyptian Military Medicine." *Journal of the Australian Defence Force Health Service*, 2009.

Stetter, Cornelius. *The Secret Medicine of the Pharaohs: Ancient Egyptian Healing*. Illinois: Quintessence Publishing Co. Inc., 1993.

Time-Life Books, and Brown, Dale (editor). *Egypt: Land of the Pharaohs*. Alexandria: The Time Inc. Book Company, 1992.

Weeks, Kent. "Valley of the Kings." *National Geographic*, September 1998.

Wilcox, Barbara. "Stanford Archaeologist Leads the First Detailed Study of Human Remains at the Ancient Egyptian Site of Deir el-Medina." *Stanford Report*, November 2014. stanford.edu/news

Williams, A.R. "Death on the Nile." *National Geographic*, October 2002.

Winer, Bart. *Life in the Ancient World*. New York: Random House, 1961.

Woods, Geraldine. *Science in Ancient Egypt*. New York: Franklin Watts, 1988.

Zivie, Alain. "A Pharaoh's Peacemaker." *National Geographic*, October 2002.

Online Articles

BBC.co.uk, "Imhotep." Accessed June 16, 2015.

Britannica.com, "Imhotep." Accessed June 16, 2015.

Egyptpast.com, "Pyramids." Accessed June 16, 2015.

Highfield, Roger. "How Imhotep Gave us Medicine." May 2007. telegraph.co.uk Accessed June 16, 2015.

History-world.org, "Imhotep." Accessed June 16, 2015.

Oakwood.edu, "Imhotep: The True Father of Medicine." Accessed June 16, 2015.

PSA.org.au, "The Ancient Egyptians, the Greeks, and the Romans." Accessed June 16, 2015.

Sullivanet.com, "Imhotep." Accessed June 16, 2015.

Vopus.org, "Imhotep, Master of Sciences." Accessed June 16, 2015.

Wikipedia, "Ancient Egyptian Medicine." Accessed June 16, 2015.

Wikipedia, "Ancient Egyptian Medicine." Accessed June 16, 2015.

Wikipedia, "Imhotep." Accessed June 16, 2015.

LEXI AND HIPPOCRATES
FIND TROUBLE AT THE OLYMPICS

A PREVIEW

To enjoy more of Lexi Catt's meowmoirs please visit your local bookstore, library, or www.megsbooks.com

Pythia predicts my future.

CHAPTER ONE

PYTHIA'S PROPHESY

The room smelled stinky as usual. The stench of rotten eggs came from steam floating out from a crack in the floor. Everyone said it was volcanic. I didn't care. Since I was born in the temple, I had come to know Pythia as a priestess who gave hope to troubled people. I liked her for that, so I spent time with her whenever I could, in spite of the stinky room where people sought her help.

On that particular day, I was enjoying a catnap on Pythia's lap. Pythia was the priestess of the Apollo Temple at Delphi. She told people what to expect in the future. She stared into space while she thought to herself and absently rubbed my ears.

Pythia's hand stopped abruptly. She spoke rapidly, "Lexi! You will soon meet a great man—a man who will influence the health of people for generations to come. Together, you and he will change lives. Go quickly to the front steps of the temple and await your destiny."

Leaping down, I scampered to the top steps so I could see my "destiny" arrive, but all I saw was a scrawny young fellow and a mangy mutt climbing the stairs.

Then, I felt a slight twitch in my tail. Me-oh-oh! I knew that meant trouble, so I prepared to spring into action.

The chase is on!

"Stay!" the young man ordered the dog. "I have to ask Pythia about my future."

The dog sat on the top step; his eyes followed his master until he disappeared into the temple.

Then, the dog turned to me, let out a low growl, and said, "Hey, mewy mouse-catcher! You are my next meal!"

I was reluctant to leave my post, but I had no choice. The chase was on! I knew the temple grounds well, so I soon lost the slow-witted mongrel in the gardens. I scampered back to the steps to await my fate. Fate hurt more than I expected.

Blinded by the afternoon sun as he stumbled out of the temple, the young man tripped over me with a nasty kick and sent himself sprawling. He rose quickly and grabbed me before I could move. With surprisingly gentle fingers, he checked to make sure I was not injured. The dog returned.

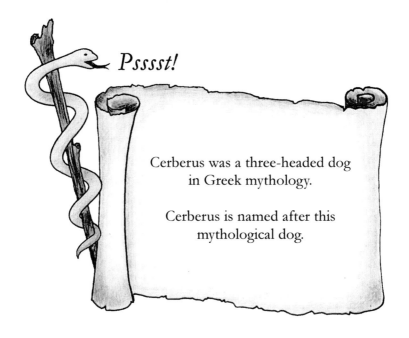

Psssst!

Cerberus was a three-headed dog in Greek mythology.

Cerberus is named after this mythological dog.

"Cerberus, stay!" The dog sat, panting heavily. "Pythia said that I must look out for the small, sick, and injured, and I must run swiftly to win. She said I would find my luck in fur but my destiny would be tied to a great man on the island of Cos. Mother told me the oracle would set my future on the right track if I followed her directions.

"So, Cerberus," Cerberus stood up expectantly, "we will go to Cos to meet a great man. I think I will bring this furry cat for extra luck."

Psssst!

Cos is a Greek island
southeast of the Greek mainland.

Cerberus drooped his head and gave me a sidelong glance. The mutt didn't look happy at this idea.

An old priest of the temple who had witnessed our accident asked as he passed by, "Are you hurt, young man?"

"No," the young man replied. "I am fine, thank you."

"Is Lexi hurt?" The priest pointed at me with his cane.

"No, the cat is fine too. Does he belong to you?"

"No. He's just one of the stray temple cats."

"Then he will be my cat now. My name is Theo."

"Good fortune to you, Theo," said the priest before he hobbled away.

Theo said to his dog, "Cerberus, this is Lexi. He's coming with us, so be a good dog and be polite to our cat."

The mongrel scowled at me and said, "That's Sir-Bear-Us to you, cat!"

And I replied, "That's Alexander Catt—with two 't's—to you, Sir, and you may call me Mister Catt! I am always polite."

So the three of us—Theo, Cerberus, and I—made our way by land and sea to the island of Cos, where we met a man so great that he is still respected for his wisdom in the twenty-first century. Hippocrates was his name!

I had never travelled before, so I expected to see new sights and to meet interesting people. However, Theo and Cerberus knew how hot, dusty, and tiring the trip would be because they were going back the way they had come, retracing their route back to the coast.

At first I scampered ahead because I was excited to travel. Theo and Cerberus laughed at my foolish efforts; it was a long, tiring walk to the coast, so they walked steadily and stopped often to rest, eat, and drink. I soon realized why they had looked so tired and dirty when they arrived at the temple in Delphi.

Many days passed before I smelled the sea. Theo and Cerberus stepped up the pace, and soon we saw docks and boats. Which boat would we travel on? Would there be fish to eat? How long would it take to reach Cos?

Theo arranged for us to travel on a local cargo boat that took supplies to the many small islands on the way to Cos. It took more than a week to sail to our destination. Cerberus slept a lot. I tried to sleep too, but my tummy rocked more than the boat! Oh, meow! I decided I would never be a sailor cat.

We listened to Hippocrates' lecture.

 Marian Keen, B.S. in Education, Central Connecticut State University, has been writing in a variety of genres since the early 1980s. Marian majored in middle-grade education, and taught grades five and six.

In *Lexi Catt's Meowmoirs—Tales of Heroic Scientists*, the talented feline Lexi shares his adventures with heroes who have made discoveries in the fields of science and medicine, including those from ancient Egypt, one of the earliest civilizations to practice medicine.

Marian's works and commentary can be found at: megsbooks.com and stresstonics.com.

Marian Keen has been writing in a variety of genres since the 1980s, with a special interest in historical fiction for children and youth.

Marian's middle-grade stories for children include the *Adventures of Alexander Catt*, and *Lexi Catt's Meowmoirs—Tales of Heroic Scientists*. These "meowmoirs" bring to life famous people and significant milestones in science, medicine, art, exploration, and human development:

- *Lexi & Hippocrates Find Trouble at the Olympics*
- *Lexi & Marie Curie Saving Lives in World War I*
- *Lexi & Lister Defeat Death*
- *Lexi & Imhotep to the Rescue!*

Look for new titles to be released soon.

Her stories for young readers feature British Columbian animals such as skunks, racoons, owls, bears, squirrels, crows, and seagulls. A complete list of works, including her poetry, can be found at megsbooks.com.

Verity, also published by Influence Publishing, is her first novel for teens.

With a life-long interest in nutrition, healthy living, and illness prevention, Marian's health articles can be found at stresstonics.com.

Jodie Dias, BA, Art History, University of British Columbia, is a children's illustrator, painter, designer, and photographer. Her whimsical style brings life to *Lexi Catt's Meowmoirs—Tales of Heroic Scientists*. Her previous works include *Lexi and Hippocrates Find Trouble at the Olympics*; *Lexi and Marie Curie Saving Lives in WWI*; *Lexi and Lister Defeat Death*; *Abigail Skunk's Lessons for Her Kits*; and *Alexander Catt's Kitty Letters for Kids*. In the Lexi Series, Jodie's playful imagery is set in historically accurate settings.

She was production manager for the children's animated movie, *Legend of the Candy Cane*; partner and graphic designer with Keen Designs; and a commissioned portrait artist.

Wendy Watson, BFA, University of Victoria, is a visual artist, designer, wood-block print maker, watercolour painter, and professional photographer with superb production and finishing techniques. Her children's illustrative works include *Lexi and Hippocrates Find Trouble at the Olympics*; *Lexi and Marie Curie Saving Lives in WWI*; *Lexi and Lister Defeat Death*; and *Abigail Skunk's Lessons for Her Kits*.

Her works have been shown in many Vancouver-area galleries; she was a partner and designer with Keen Designs; she is a commissioned artist; and she currently works at Langara College.

If you want to get on the path to becoming a published author with Influence Publishing please go to www.InfluencePublishing.com

inspiring books that influence change

More information on our other titles and how to submit your own proposal can be found at www.InfluencePublishing.com

CPSIA information can be obtained at www.ICGtesting.com
Printed in the USA
LVOW08s1532301215

468277LV00010B/78/P